M000197408

Also by Nate Southard:

Pale Horses
Down
Just Like Hell
Red Sky
Lights Out

A Broken River Books collection

Broken River Books
10765 SW Murdock Lane
Apt. G6
Tigard, OR 97224

Copyright: *Deeper Waters* © 2009, Nate Southard
He Stepped Through © 2010, Nate Southard
Something Went Wrong © 2012, Nate Southard
Safe House © 2014, Nate Southard

Cover art and design copyright © 2015 by Matthew Revert
www.matthewrevert.com

Interior design by J David Osborne

All rights reserved. No part of this book may be reproduced or transmitted in any form or by any means, electronic or mechanical, including photocopying, recording, or by any information storage and retrieval system, without the written consent of the publisher, except where permitted by law.

This is a work of fiction. All names, characters, places, and incidents are the product of the author's imagination. Where the names of actual celebrities or corporate entities appear, they are used for fictional purposes and do not constitute assertions of fact. Any resemblance to real events or persons, living or dead, is coincidental.

ISBN: 978-1-940885-23-0

Printed in the USA.

WILL THE SUN EVER COME OUT AGAIN?

NATE SOUTHARD

BROKEN RIVER BOOKS
PORTLAND, OR

This one's for Heather Harper Ellett.
Friend.
Lifeline.
Guardian of the Chai.
Wearer of cute shoes.

TABLE OF CONTENTS

TO
THE FEARLESS
ONES

an introduction by
Laird Barron

Nate Southard pinged my radar screen a few years ago with a brutal novella called *Just Like Hell*. That story caused a ripple in the horror community for the high-quality of the writing and a layered approach to sex and violence often lacking in literature. After reading *Just Like Hell* and a follow-up collection, *Broken Skin*, I added him onto my list of hard-nosed literary bruisers. The gunslingers. The blue-collar crowd. His work appealed to me on a fundamental level--structured with deceptive ease that belies a universe of nuance, and refreshingly unimpaired by the stranglehold Judeo-Christian mythology exerts upon the horror genre.

If you think you know someone from a handful of early-career stories, you're being setup for a surprise. Southard arrived on the scene with the poise and capability of a veteran. That's a rare accomplishment. What's rarer is the kind of writer he's matured into.

Yes, he's tough as leather. He doesn't pull his punches, he doesn't flinch from the harsh truth, and he doesn't coddle his characters or the reader. And no, he isn't constrained by the usual paradigms. What Southard is, is one of the hardest

1

working writers tilling the field. He's a maestro in the art of lo-fi blood in your eye horror, psycho-slasher creepiness. That's only the beginning of the particular madness he's laying down: Horror is merely a sample of his palette. His narratives pitch into crime, science fiction, and pulp noir with admirable facility.

I possess a fondness for the Ellroy/Thompson end of the spectrum--scotch, lead, and femmes fatals, and so does Southard. His words smell of gun smoke that follows five rounds and whips of sparks through the barrel of a .41 magnum. He captures the reek of flop sweat and the baritone drone of murderous bastards talking themselves into another killing. He drives a story with steely-eyed recklessness down night-roads, tires screaming, headlights out, strange silhouettes rearranging through a windshield smashed to hell in a spider web of cracks.

Authors are in dialogue with their colleagues, living and dead. Everybody in this business is a product of his or her influences. The best flare with something like anger, more complicated, though, and after they've read enough and lived enough they say, *enough*, and push back, or punch up as if they've got something to prove, as if something vital is in the balance, as if something dear is on the line. Comparing his style to contemporaries, Southard slugs like Donald Ray Pollack, switches and jabs like Norman Partridge, but his angles are unorthodox and peculiar like a postmodernist stepped back to 1937 and said, "Mr. Lovecraft, before you go, there's something I need to ask…"

It's an admirable thing to chop against the grain, to be unafraid and unabashed regarding one's affection for the grimy, pulpy roots of horror and suspense. Far too often for my taste, writers flee the influences that shaped them. Some taste commercial success, or heaven forfend, receive laurels from literary critics, and promptly disavow provenance. *I'm not a horror writer!* cries the author who built her success on multiple horror novels and collections. *I don't write science fiction,* demurs the novelist who made his bones with dystopian yarns featuring super science and time travel. It's a knock on genre, of course. It's tantamount to saying that the genus that spawned them is a slumming ground; *real* art lies elsewhere. I admire those who reject such craven impulses. We live in a world that gave us the pulp genius of Robert E. Howard, the feminist retrofitting of fairytales by Angela Carter, and currently the visceral dark fantasy of Livia Llewellyn; each a wordsmith, each committed to artistry with such ferocious devotion that reading them for the first time is a shock to the senses, an experience that nicks the psyche.

The greatest and bravest artists are all in to the last chip, equivocations notwithstanding. Give me an honest heart, such as Ramsey Campbell's, any day. Give me a writer who says, *this is where I come from and this is what I do.* Give me a straight-shooter such as the aforementioned Norman Partridge. Give me Nate Southard.

Presumably, I've provided you an inkling of what you're in for just over the rise. There's blood and violence in the offing. Sex and eeriness. Plain old weirdness with a capital W, too. Time-shifting vampires. Sinister black-ops agencies and the ruthless fixers who inhabit them. Home-grown terrorist cells versus primordial evil. Madness and mayhem undulates through the soft membrane of space-time. You will behold the unholy physiognomy of a dark god. You will fall beneath the shadow of immense and implacable mysteries.

Real human beings struggle amidst and against these forces. The greatest virtue of Southard's blue-collar aesthetic lies in its authenticity. The pain is true. The suffering and the terror are true. So is the tenderness, the longing, the blood and the tears shed. Horror is powerless in a vacuum. Terror is wasted on cardboard dolls. Drama cannot exist if the actors are false, if the stakes are nonexistent. A writer who ventures into this dark corner of the imagination must surely know a bit about the darkness of the soul. He or she must comprehend how dread exerts influence upon the mind, how loss and bitterness poison the spirit. That writer must indulge the vicissitudes of raw emotion without succumbing. That writer must experience fear, passionately and profoundly, yet forge onward, a faithful interpreter of nightmares. That writer must be a fearless one.

Serendipitously for this field that I so cherish, we are honored with the contributions of bright lights such as Nathan Southard. He is wise in the ways of the heart. He knows storytelling is nothing without it.

—Laird Barron
Rifton, NY
December 18, 2014

HE STEPPED THROUGH

MORNING

"Yo, Loop. Ready for this shit?"

Loop stares at his lap and giggles. B-Dawg gets it, but he needs homeboy on the clock. It's business time.

"Loop?"

Homeboy stops giggling and checks out the scenery like it matters one fuck. "It's cloudy. Ain't been this cloudy in a long time."

"Asked if you ready."

"Will the sun ever come out again?"

"Loop."

"I'm cool."

"Sure?"

"Fuck, yeah."

"Good. We here. Let's do it."

"He stepped through?"

"He stepped through."

Regina carries the plastic tray away from the counter and over to the booth where Carl and Shay bounce like nothing in the world can ever tire them. Cartoon smiles stretch across their faces, and both cheer when they see the tray. She likes that. Makes her feel wanted.

"Breakfast!" Shay cries.

"That's right." She sets down the tray and slides into the booth beside Carl. She has to sit next to him. Otherwise, he might lose interest in the meal and wander off. So long as she blocks the empty space beneath the table with her legs, she can control him. "Let's see what we got. Sausage biscuit and OJ for Shay, bacon and eggs for Carl."

"I don't want eggs."

"You wanted 'em a minute ago."

"That was then. Now I don't want 'em."

"Well, now I paid for 'em, so you gonna eat 'em."

"No."

"Don't test me. We don't get to do this every day. Now eat so I won't have to tan your little ass when we get home."

"Damn."

"You watch that mouth, Carl. Don't make me tell you again."

She sets a chocolate milk in front of her son and then turns to her own meal. The wax paper wrapping her sausage and egg is already slick with grease. She wads up the wrapper and drops it to the tray. The first bite of her biscuit tastes just fine, not at all like chalk or dirt. They taste that way sometimes.

Something squeals on the street. She looks up from the table as a Lincoln bounces off Alondra Boulevard and into the parking lot. Whoever is driving doesn't bother parking, just brings the ride to a smoking halt in the driveway. The maneuver jumps her heart, tells her the driver's either looking for fun or violence.

The Lincoln's doors open, and two men climb out. She recognizes their colors. Gray Street Bangers.

"No."

Regina grabs Carl's hand, reaches across the table for Shay's. They yell something as she starts to drag them from the booth, but then one of the bangers kicks open the door and their voices disappear, trampled under a stampede of screams.

"Little early in the morning for a prime-time style clusterfuck."

Walker rolls his neck left and then right. A real bastard of a headache throbs at the base of his skull, and the motion doesn't help the way he hoped. Perfect. "You know the bangers. No respect for a man's schedule."

"No shit. At least let me get through a fucking coffee." Rawls' voice is a low rumble, the sort of sound that might set off an earthquake. He tries to take a sip from the paper cup in his grip, but a pothole sends it sloshing over his hand instead. He hisses and shakes off a few drops, licks his fingers.

"Classy," Walker says through the thinnest of grins. "You're just classy all the way from your dick to your asshole."

"Fuck you. You could drive, I wouldn't have this problem."

"Tell yourself that. See where it gets ya."

"How about you just get us to the scene without planting us in a brick wall?"

9

"See what I can do." He tears through the intersection of Alondra and Harris and then gives the car more gas. Two blocks, then he'll see what kind of shithole he gets to spend the morning digging out.

Another day on the job. Hooray.

Regina hugs her babies to her chest and squeezes her eyes shut. Two more shots pop off, and the pack of screams grows a little thinner. Shay squirms against her side, sobbing. Carl remains quiet. He just lays there like he's sleeping. Brave boy. Her brave little man.

One of the Gray Street boys keeps giggling. It's a high, tittering sound that sets her teeth chattering and her body shivering. Sounds like a basehead on a bad fix. He was the one who started shooting. Just came through the door blasting and laughing. Her memory replays the teenage girl behind the counter and the way the back of her head blasted all over the food bin. Her eyes were still open when she fell, a look like a question shining in them.

"It'll be okay," Regina whispers to her babies. She doesn't know if they can even hear her, but she doesn't dare raise her voice. Last thing she wants is to attract attention.

Something crashes, and her entire body jumps. She opens her eyes and sees the other banger has kicked over one of the garbage cans. Half-empty cups spill their remaining contents, soda and orange juice mixing with a fan of paper wrappers and styrofoam containers.

The culprit jumps on top of the can's enclosure and swings a pistol in a wide arc. The black metal fills her world.

"Who next?" the man yells. His voice sounds hollow, like he's talking from the bottom of a deep hole.

The other keeps giggling. He stands behind the counter and drags the dead girl back to her feet. Regina sees her head appear above the counter. The laughing boy slings her over the steel surface, and something wet and gray falls out of her skull to splat across the floor.

Regina closes her eyes again. She pulls her kids as close as she can.

Why isn't Carl moving?

Walker pulls the car over half a block from the fast food joint. A trio of squad cars have beat them there. A pair of blues works at closing off the street, waving the traffic back toward Caress. Hopefully somebody can set up some fucking saw horses soon. They don't need to be wasting good uniforms on traffic detail.

He climbs out of the car and chases after Rawls. The redwood of a man is already chest to nose with the nearest blue.

"What are we looking at?"

"Two Gray Streets walked into the Edgar's on the corner of Muriel and lit the place up."

"Anybody get out?" Walker asks.

"Don't know."

"We just know they're armed."

"Yeah, and there's two of them."

"Hostages?"

"Yeah."

Rawls shoots the uni a look. "How many?"

"Oh. Don't know. Not quite the morning rush hour, so…"

"How many dead?" Walker asks. Impatience grows in him like a fever.

"Don't know."

"Thanks. You're a testament to good police."

A flash of anger in the kid's eyes, but shame too. Fine. Maybe he'll learn something.

Walker steps away, motions for Rawls to join him. He hears more sirens approaching, at least two.

"How you feeling?" he asks his partner.

"Pretty good." Rawls shrugs. His thick shoulders stretch the T-shirt he wears. Gang Unit has a few perks, and ditching a suit every goddamn day sits in the top three.

"Any thoughts?"

"Gray Street turf. No reason for boys to be going apeshit. They been quiet for weeks now."

"Better to make some noise."

"In their own back yard?"

"Maybe some Locos wandered in, wanted to wave their balls around."

"Doesn't feel right."

"No, it doesn't."

Walker breathes deep. Compton stinks to high fuck most days, and today is anything but an exception. The scents of hot tar and old grease fill his nose like a wad of dirty cotton. After nearly five years he thinks he should be used to it, but it never gets any better. It settles in his lungs and starts to rot. Maybe it will eat him up like cancer some day.

"So you wanna wait for SWAT?"

Rawls grins. "Not really."

"We can cut through some yards, come up from the rear."

"Sounds like a plan."

"Tell the babies. Then we're moving."

"You! Open your eyes."

Regina hears the command but doesn't obey. If she doesn't follow, then he can't be talking to her. It's somebody else. Plenty of people still screaming. He's talking to one of them, not her. Never her.

"Bitch, I told you open your damn eyes. Don't make me cut 'em open."

She hears footsteps, paper cups skittering across dirty tile. He's not coming for her. Somebody nearby, but not—

A hand grabs her hair and jerks into a fist.

A scream rips loose from her throat as her eyes snap open. She sees the black hole of a gun barrel and nothing else. Shay cringes in her arm but Carl sits still like a good boy. He feels wet, though. Maybe he's gone and peed himself. She wants to do the same.

"Yo, bitch! You do what I damn-well say when I damn-well say it. Don't go pissing me off!"

She hears a whimper deep in her throat and she hates herself for it. She's been telling herself for years that she ain't afraid of these Gray Street punks, and now here she is, making baby sounds. She tries to screw up her face into a defiant sneer, but her jaw trembles. Her lips quiver. Tears sting at her eyes.

She hates herself, but she's too scared to do anything other than stare into the black hole of the gun's barrel.

Shay pulls tighter, arms cinching around her neck. The world swims around her. The black hole wavers and then grows. The other Gray Street boy keeps giggling in the background, and she hears a new noise, something wet and ripping. She tries to place the sound, but her thoughts are too heavy and slow, the black hole too wide.

Maybe she'll go to sleep. That could be okay. She won't be afraid there.

The fist in her hair jerks again, and another scream wakes her. The angry hand disappears, only to return as a slap across her face. Somehow, the attack convinces Regina to ease up, and her breath returns in a cold, stinking rush.

"Look at me, bitch!"

She does her best, fighting for focus, trying to see something other than the black hole. She finds a face and takes inventory of its features. The lips twist into a sneer. The nostrils flare and blow hot breath. The eyes burn with something she hasn't seen before. There's anger in there, but something else too. It's not the posturing she's seen before from these Gray Street boys. This is something worse. It swirls out of control, casting shadows, and she thinks it might be insanity.

"What?" she asks. Her voice is so quiet she's not sure she really said anything. Maybe it was just a thought.

The Gray Street Banger fumes at her for a moment, and the world goes silent until he speaks.

"Gimme the boy."

Walker hops a chain link fence and jogs across a stranger's backyard. A jangling sound tells him Rawls is right behind. Not too hot yet, but the Kevlar vest draws sweat from his pores. He already has his service piece drawn and ready to rock. Half a block until he even needs it, but he sure as shit doesn't want to leave the hardware holstered while jumping fences in the middle of Compton.

A woman wearing only an oversized T-shirt storms out of a sliding glass door as he reaches the yard's opposite side. He throws a look over his shoulder and sees the rage in her movements, in the explosive look on her face.

"Muthafuckas, get out my fuckin' yard!"

He hears Rawls spit a quick, "LAPD!" and then he's over the fence and into the next yard. Toys here. A rusted bicycle. A plastic laser pistol bleached by the sun. Half-inflated football. He wonders if they've been touched in the last year, if the kid who owned them is even a kid anymore, even alive. Maybe the owner grew up to be a Gray Streeter. Maybe he got caught in a drive-by and took a round in the chest or face. Thousand ways to die in this hellhole, and he's seen damn near every one.

Thank God for the perks. The extra cash might not be official, but it sure does come in handy. Spends as easy as any other cash, too. He thinks the perks are the only thing keeping him from saying 'fuck it,' leaving the force and working private security. Pretty good money in that, he's heard. Gotta wear a suit, sure, but shadowing some teen pop star with a tight ass can't be too tough.

Probably wouldn't get to go knock around a couple of bangers blasting up an Edgar's, though.

* * *

"You don't touch my boy!"

The black hole hovers in front of her face, but Regina doesn't care anymore. She isn't going to let this psychopath take her Carl. Shay, neither. She holds her kids tight against her chest. The banger's words have made Carl go completely limp, and that pisses her off. You don't go scaring a working woman's kids.

She scowls at the Gray Street piece of trash. If the black hole would go away, she'd climb to her feet and beat this punk-ass senseless. She'd teach him something about respect. Real respect, not that gangsta shit the dumb ass niggas coming up care about so much.

You don't scare her kids.

"Fuck you," she says.

He stares at her for a second, and somewhere behind the black hole she can see the confusion twisting with the insanity in his eyes. People don't disobey him, haven't for a long time. For a second she worries that she's given him an excuse to pull the trigger, but then she decides she doesn't care. This limp-dick motherfucker isn't taking her son.

The black hole disappears. The Gray Streeter lowers the pistol, and Regina almost smiles. Then something barks. A force like dual hammers takes out her eardrums in the same instant something punches her in the stomach. She folds toward the greasy tile, and her arms go limp. She tries to tighten them again, to hold her kids close to her and tell them everything will be okay, but she can't find any strength.

Sound starts to return. She hears a new round of screams, and somewhere far away she hears the ripping noises. She wonders what they might be, but she doesn't want to raise her head to check. She wants to stay low to the ground.

Her stomach alternates between freezing and burning, and she thinks she's never felt anything like this before. She doesn't like it. Not one little bit.

He did it, she thinks. *Big man went and pulled that trigger.*

Something brushes against her stinging ear, an insect that wants to burrow in and create a new home. She hisses through grit teeth, and she realizes the insect is Shay whimpering in her ear.

"Mommy, Mommy, Mommy."

It's okay, baby. Everything will be okay. Mommy just needs to plug the hole in her belly.

Something is pulled from her grip. It's limp and wet and cooling, and she doesn't realize it's Carl until he's gone and she's holding stagnant air.

"No!" The word comes out like a roar. It sends an explosion of pure agony through her system. Her cheek rests against the floor, and she feels something hot and thick touch her face. She knows it's her blood, but the realization doesn't make much difference.

I'm sorry, babies. I'm sorry. I'm sorry. I'm—

The pistol barks again.

Walker hits the parking lot at a run. He glances over his shoulder and sees Rawls coming over the last fence. His partner throws him a nod, and together they race toward the restaurant.

They approach the structure from the rear. Walker looks at the faded brick and sees the first body. It's a teenager, male, splayed out in the open back door with a pool of blood collecting around him. As he closes in, he makes out a hole the size of a fingertip in the kid's back. He knows there's probably a wound as big as a fist in the poor bastard's chest. Kid never had a chance.

At least it gives them a way inside.

He thumbs his radio, speaks into his shoulder. "Approaching from southeast corner. At least one civilian down. EMTs required." He speaks quietly, but he still feels a tightening in his gut as he wonders if the bangers inside can hear him. He clicks off the radio in order to eliminate any incoming surprises.

He wonders if the shooters are people he knows. That could cause problems. Nothing he can't handle, but he doesn't like complications.

He closes to within ten feet of the door, his pistol now up and aimed at the open space between the steel and brick. His senses reach out. His hearing pulls in all surrounding information, and his brain sorts the city noise from the closer sounds. He hears a few muffled screams, something that might be laughter, high and shrill. He looks for shadows, any sign of movement, finds nothing.

He presses his back to the bricks beside the doorway. His heart accelerates. He's used to the response, almost relishes it. He draws upon an inner calm to balance it. He's been in dangerous situations before. He's talked his way out of some and shot his way out of others. This is just the next one in line.

18

He feels Rawls fall in place beside him. "If it's one of ours?" the big man asks.

"Drop him. No need to take a risk."

"Amen."

"Ready?"

Rawls nods. He shows no emotion. His face is a concrete mask. His eyes are dark pools full of secrets. Walker knows he looks the same.

He gives the body at his feet a glance, and then he steps over it. He plants a foot between its sprawled legs, careful to avoid the blood that's spilled. In the space of a heartbeat he slides through the door and presses his back to an interior wall. No gunshots greet him, and he figures that's as lucky as he'll get today.

A steel industrial sink stands against the back wall to his left, a walk-in freezer dead ahead. A pile of folded cardboard boxes separates him from a row of steel shelves that hold bags of hamburger buns. He can't see the grill, let alone the front of the store. He can definitely hear screams, though. There's giggling, too. Great. Angel dust or meth. Either one means he's dealing with psychopaths.

He darts across to press himself against the freezer as Rawls enters behind him. He catches a glimpse of the kitchen as he makes the move, and the smell hits him a second later. It wrinkles his nose and almost distracts him. He can tell it's supposed to be a comforting smell, a breakfast scent. Instead, it stinks like lard left in a skillet until it turns black and smokes. He flashes back to the summer he spent working in a hamburger joint, the long showers to scrape the rotten smell of grease and mustard from his skin, the burns from popping

19

beef fat and flat grills that should be hauled away by the government as public hazards. Getting shot at by bangers feels pretty good in comparison. At least one gets you laid.

He ducks low and waves for Rawls to follow. He senses his partner pulling away from the wall, and he inches his way into the kitchen.

Loop can't stop giggling, but he don't give a damn. He works on the dead bitch with a smile in his goddamn heart. He don't even really know what he's doing to her. He sure as hell don't know how she got that hole in the back of her skull. Looks like the motherfucking thing exploded. Like a nigga stashed a hand grenade in her dome.

He hears folks yelling and B-Dawg talking about some shit, but it all sounds far away. It don't concern him none. Got his own shit right here, his own little world. It ain't as big as the real world, but it's just as pretty.

He holds a tool in his hand, but he can't remember the word for it. It's sharp. He knows that much. It moved through the dead bitch with no trouble at all. He reaches inside and pulls the squishy stuff out. It feels good, but he don't think that makes a big never mind no more. Everything be new in the hood now. Ain't nothing gonna be the same again. Not after last night.

A phrase rolls through his head like a bass line.

He stepped through. He stepped through. He stepped through.

* * *

Sporadic screams punctuate the journey from the back of the store into the kitchen. They sound beyond scared, crossing the line into hysterical. Walker thinks the stretches of silence are worse, though. When it goes quiet he can hear other things, like the giggling and a second voice muttering rapid syllables. There's another sound, too. It takes him a second to figure it out, but once he realizes what the ripping sound followed by wet splats must be he knows this is a call unlike any he's ever seen.

He hears a nearly-silent whimper to his left, and he swings the pistol around as he moves his eyes. He finds a teenage boy, a skinny thing with eyes the size of golf balls and a tremble born of horror in his limbs. Walker puts a finger to his lips and prays the kid knows well enough to do as he's told. The kid gives him a look that says *Please get me out of here.* Walker shakes his head. Can't risk it, not with two psychos within fifty feet of the kitchen. He turns away before the kid starts crying.

He jumps when a finger taps his shoulder. He thinks it might be the kid, that this whole thing just got a lot harder and a lot more aggravating. He shoots an angry look over his shoulder, finds Rawls. He asks a question with his eyes, and Rawls jerks a thumb back and up.

A mirror. It hangs on the kitchen's rear wall just below the ceiling. To the customers waiting in line for their grease-saturated burgers, it would provide a view of the cooks fussing around between the grill and warmers and deep fryers. From Walker's crouched position, he can see the front counter and a good portion of the dining room.

He doesn't like what he sees.

Two homeboys. The witnesses got that much right. Their colors say Gray Street. One stands at the counter, slashing at a body with a knife. The jumping of his shoulders marks him as the giggler. The body might have been a girl once. Now it's a mess.

The other banger is crouched over something in the dining room. It looks like he's got his piece jammed in the back of his jeans, but Walker can't tell for sure. His eyes keep pulling away to the bodies that litter the floor like wreckage. He counts five in addition to the girl spread across the registers like a science experiment.

His eyes move to Rawls. His partner shakes his head. He doesn't like it, either. If there's any bright side, it's that neither of the bangers looks like one of theirs. It's not much of a comfort, but it helps.

He gives Rawls a nod, and together they move to the edge of the warmer. He leans around so that he can see the asshole with the laughter problem. The guy looks older than your average New Jack. Probably been in for awhile now. Should be smarter than something like this. The giggling makes Walker want to think the guy's sailing. Something about it doesn't sit right, though. He's seen plenty of fiends over the years, and none of them have sounded like this. This guy just sounds crazy. His tittering grabs Walker by the spine and squeezes, chills him. It certainly fits with the banger's little hobby.

Walker tries to watch as the Gray Streeter works on the dead girl. He sees the blade—a butcher knife longer than the average forearm—rise and fall. He has to turn his head when the man pulls a thick loop of intestine from the girl's opened torso and flings it down the counter's length. He still hears the fleshy smack of the girl's innards slapping the counter. The sound tells him it's time to stop this.

He rises to his full height and whips around the warmer in the same instant. He brings his pistol up and locks it on the banger's head. He knows Rawls will cover the Gray Streeter crouching in the dining room. In the space of a breath he takes a single step forward.

"*Freeze!* LAPD!"

A round of screams fills the restaurant, but it doesn't faze him. His eyes don't leave the man with the knife; his aim doesn't waver. He's good at this, one of the few things in life he can make work.

The giggler doesn't stop, doesn't even acknowledge Walker. He keeps working on the thing that used to be a girl and is now just a sloppy pile of meat and blood and bone. The arm moves in spastic jerks. The blade dives, rips, pulls free. Walker focuses on the psycho, refuses to look at the girl. There's nothing he can do for her. Right now he has to get this crazed banger under control before somebody else gets hurt.

"Hey, asshole. I'm talking to you, here. Drop the weapon and put your hands behind your head."

No response. The psycho keeps hacking away, probably lost deep inside his head.

"*Yo!*"

For some reason, the word gets through. Walker sees the giggler twitch. Something flashes through the banger's eyes. He whirls, bringing the knife around like a sword. Walker jerks back even though the Gray

Street boy is still at least ten feet away. He sees the dark shadow of madness in the man's eyes, but then the blade slashes again, and he pulls the trigger.

The bullet enters the banger's face just below the left eye. Walker charges forward as the back of the man's head erupts and his body slumps to the bloody tile. He kicks the knife from fingers that still grip because they don't know they're already dead. He refuses to take chances with this psycho. The blade clatters across the ground as it disappears beneath the warmer. Good. A uni can dig it out later.

"Walker!"

He turns toward Rawls' voice and sees his partner standing over the remaining banger, piece trained on the man's temple. Rawls doesn't look up from the man he has covered, doesn't so much as glance in another direction. He's good, always has been.

Walker sees something in his eyes, though. There's too much white there, and they nearly vibrate in their sockets. His face has gone pale and tight. Walker knows horror when he sees it. Maybe the mess on the counter is catching up to Rawls, but Walker doubts it. Something has gone wrong.

He gives the giggler a final look just to make sure he's not getting up, and then he rushes around the counter. He moves with practiced care, his feet avoiding every spatter of blood, keeping the crime scene intact.

As he enters the dining room he hears a soft sound, something meaty and moist. Chewing. Did this drugged out piece of shit decide he was hungry and start chomping on a breakfast sandwich? The thought angers Walker. He sees himself pistol-whipping the banger to sleep, writing it up as resisting or threatening an officer. Serves this asshole right for going on a killing spree just to grab a snack.

But that doesn't explain the look on Rawls' face. As Walker steps closer, his pistol trained on the lone Gray Streeter's back, he sees the tiny legs. They lay twisted clumsily, peeking out from in front of the hunched banger. They're a puzzle piece he doesn't like. The dead woman lying face down a few feet away and the little girl staring and trembling are other pieces, and he hates them just as much. He hates that chewing sound most of all, though. He can't make sense of it, and it eats away at his patience. It disintegrates his dwindling sense that everything will be okay.

He creeps closer, avoiding paper cups, greasy wrappers, and streaks of fresh blood. He keeps his eyes on the killer's back. He feels it's safe to not call the man a suspect. The piece remains in the man's waistband, and the chewing sound grows louder. He wonders if a kick to the back of the banger's skull would make it stop. Instead he inches forward until he can touch the man. He sees the man has his hands to his mouth, but he instead concentrates on the pistol. He reaches forward slowly. When his fingers are within inches of the piece, he snatches it from the waistband.

The banger's unarmed, but he doesn't find it comforting. Instead, he just wants to know what the hell the piece of shit is chewing on.

"Walker," Rawls says. His voice sounds sick. "Look."

He slides the weapon into his holster as he steps to the left. He keeps his own pistol trained on the man's skull. As he moves, he sees the rest of the tiny body attached to the twisted legs. A little boy with crumbs from a breakfast biscuit on his fingers. Glassy eyes stare at the ceiling. A T-shirt lies in tatters around his shoulders.

"Holy shit." He can't stop the words from tumbling past his lips.

There's a hole just below the child's sternum, a ragged opening surrounded by blood. Walker sees no knife, no cutting tool of any kind, but he knows the banger got in there somehow. Because that's the only way he could have retrieved the small heart he now holds to his mouth.

"Put it down," he tells the psychopath. "Put it right the fuck down."

He doesn't expect the Gray Street boy to obey—to even pay attention—but the man chews noisily for a second and then swallows. The man pulls the half-eaten organ away from his mouth and smiles, a terrible expression smeared with thick blood.

"He stepped through."

NOON

2Bit wakes up with bricks in his head. He thinks his skull might split open, it hurts so bad. He moves to roll off his mattress and realizes he's on the floor, his back against peeling linoleum. He wonders how he got there.

"Muthafuck." The word sends a spike of pain through his head. "Muthafuck" is right. He can't remember the last time his skull hurt like this. Course, he can't remember how the fuck he ended up on a hard floor or where he is or even what the hell he did last night. He don't like that. It gets him scared, and he hates being scared.

He groans as he rolls onto his belly and pushes himself off the floor. He don't recognize this place. It's a kitchen, but the shitty state of it means it could be anywhere in Compton. He just knows he don't recognize it.

Light stabs through a torn shade above a sink without a faucet. Must be pretty late. That's cool. 2Bit don't wake up before eleven most days. Let them business muthafuckas get up and go to work. He can sell his smoke day or night. Don't make a never mind.

He stretches his arms and legs. The knots in his muscles call him a bastard. He fights back, gets them to fall in line. A yawn follows, and somewhere in the middle of that big breath he catches a whiff of something that makes him want to hit his knees and cough up the breakfast he ain't ate yet.

"What the fuck?" He puts a hand to his nose to block out some of the stink. The whole house smells like a dead dog on a sunny day, only worse, like some brutha's been stocking up on rotting mutts. His hand smells bad, too. And it's kinda sticky. He pulls it away and sees the drying blood in his palm. It covers his hands, the stuff darker in the creases of his knuckles. What the hell? What did he do last night? He don't remember any of this shit.

He decides he needs to leave. More than anything else, he needs to get the fuck out of this place and get back to his mom's house. He can wash up there, maybe head out and see what he got himself up to. More than anything, though, he needs to get gone.

He looks for an exit. There's a pot on a blackened stove. A whirlwind of flies hovers over it, and their droning tickles his ears. He knows he don't want to see what's in the pot. He knows he won't like it. Just get out, get gone. 2Bit don't give a shit about nothing else.

He finds a doorway out of the kitchen, and he rushes through it. He moves in a stumbling run. His arms and legs fight him for control. He can't remember a time he's felt this way.

He reaches the living room and stops cold. He stares at the mess there and tries to make sense of it. What happened here? Did he do this? Did Gray Street? What the fuck?

He looks down at his hands. A lot of blood there.

He wraps his hands in his shirt and wrestles the front door open. He runs.

"Last time I checked, Gray Street were a bunch of gangbangers, not a cult of cannibals." Walker stands in a corner of the Big Room with Rawls and Captain Thomas. Cops mill around without paying much attention. The morning's shit storm keeps most of the station busy, and the desks at Walker's back remain empty.

"Well, it looks like something's changed."

"Could be something new on the street," Rawls says. "Gray Street deals like everybody else. Maybe they tried to cut their H with something and got folks freaking out."

"How many Gray Streeters use their own stash?" Thomas asks.

"One or two, tops," Walker says. He throws the tiniest glance at Rawls. Wants to make sure his partner is following along. "They're profit oriented."

"Were these two known players?"

"Neither looked young enough to be newbies, but I hadn't seen them before."

"So maybe this was an initiation?"

"Jesus, I hope not. You ask me, that wasn't an initiation. That thing was a slaughter. Six dead, and I don't even need to tell you about the rest."

"No, you don't."

"Hungry Heart say anything on the way in?"

"Not one word, according to the uniforms. They put him in interrogation room four."

"Great." He gives his partner a slap on the arm. "You want first crack?"

"Sure thing," Rawls says. His rumbling voice doesn't say anything that doesn't need saying. Thomas shakes his head a little but keeps quiet. He knows how Rawls works. He might not like it, but he knows it gets results. Sometimes that's good enough.

"What was it the suspect said on the scene?" Thomas asks.

"'He stepped through.' That's it, and that's all. Clammed up nice and tight after that."

"Mean anything to you?"

"Could mean somebody new's in charge of Gray Street. Stepped through the ranks? We haven't heard any noise, but it makes a lot of sense. New leadership wants to shake things up, put on a show and display their balls to all of Compton."

Thomas nods. The look on his face tells Walker he's proud to have any shred he can use. Rawls almost looks sad as he throws a kink in the whole thing.

"But then there's Malcolm Dobbs. He's been running Gray Street for going on five years now, and that man's a tiger. Outside of him driving a car into a phone pole, I don't see him just giving up the reigns without making enough ruckus to draw the National Guard."

"Fuck." Thomas follows it from a sigh, and suddenly he looks like he could use a month or so of sleep.

Walker knows the feeling. He wonders if he could remember the last time he didn't feel that way. Maybe if he thought about it hard enough.

"You got any cages you can rattle?" Thomas asks.

"Sure. I got a few CI's in the Gray Street organization. Might take some time to get in contact, though."

"How long?"

"Day or two at the most."

"Do better. If Dobbs or some successor is responsible for this shit, I want LAPD to roll on him by nightfall."

Walker looks to Rawls, receives a shrug. *Thanks for the assist, buddy.* "I'll see how it goes."

"I mean it. Don't drag ass on me."

"Never do, Captain." He gives his boss a look that's somewhere between sincere and shit-eating. He gives Rawls a pat on the back, one that's just hard enough to tell the guy to lean on the prick up in interrogation four good and heavy. Then, he turns on his heel and saunters back into the sunshine.

"Shit to do," he whispers on his way out the door.

Officer Megan Ricks shuts down the cruiser and shoulders open her door. She hears Christian's door open. Normally, she'd remove her shades now. She likes to look people in the eye when she talks to them. The sun is hiding behind a layer of clouds that alternates between dark gray and black, though. No shades today. She's been waiting for it to storm, but the rain feels like hiding some more.

"Tease," she says.

"What?" Christian asks. He slides his nightstick into its leather loop. His uniform stretches tight across his

31

chest, and Megan thinks again that she should really stop paying so much attention to it.

"Weather. We can use the rain, but it doesn't want to come."

"It'll come," he says. He gives her a smile that melts her a little. She likes it when he smiles. She returns the expression, and then she walks past him toward the faded green house. The street is quiet as she approaches the front door. The doorbell is nothing but a twist of wires, so she pulls open the screen and gives the door three raps with her knuckles.

"Mrs. Yarbrough? LAPD."

A raspy voice approaches from the other side of the door. She catches the words, "About time," but can't make out the rest. Sorry lady, but with all the actual crime taking place in Los Angeles, bad smells and the like take a while to filter to the top.

The door opens, and a withered black woman looks at her with narrow eyes.

"I'm Mrs. Yarbrough."

"Yes, ma'am. We received a call about a suspicious odor coming from next door?"

"More than two hours ago. Little girl, I got syrup don't take its own sweet time like you."

"I'm sorry about the delay, ma'am." She feels Christian turn away to face the street, and she knows he's smirking, trying to contain a chuckle. She longs for the luxury of turning away, but she has to deal with Mrs. Yarbrough and her mystery odor.

"You been here twenty minutes earlier, you might coulda caught the boy was inside."

"Excuse me? Somebody exited the residence?"

"Like the devil was biting his backside. Ran right up the street. Fast, too."

"About twenty minutes ago?"

"Yes."

"Did he look frightened?"

"Little girl, that boy looked terrified."

She glances at Christian. Her partner raises his eyebrows for an instant. Worth checking into.

"And which is the house in question?"

Mrs. Yarbrough squints, and her eyes nearly disappear completely. She points to her right, indicating the house next door.

Megan follows the old woman's finger and sees a house that might have been white back in the sixties or seventies. Now it's a color she imagines ashes would be if they could rot. A rusted chain link fence separates the two properties, but wild grass tall enough for a child to hide in looms through the diamond-shaped spaces as though it's hungry and wants to snatch whichever poor fool wanders too close. She tells herself she's seen plenty of homes like this in the city, but something about this one pulls at her. She can almost hear it whispering in her ear, daring her to approach.

A breeze rustles the grass, and for an instant she can smell something. It's a thick, meaty scent. It tickles her brain with cold fingers. She hopes she's imagining things, but she doubts she's that lucky.

"Thank you," she says a little too loudly. "We'll check it out. Will you be available if we have any further questions?"

"Little girl, I got no place else to be."

"All right, then. Sit tight, Mrs. Yarbrough."

She gives Christian a nod, and he follows her away from the door. As she walks toward the house with the wild yard, she thinks the city is unnaturally still. Compton's one of the last places in the country where the kids are too poor to do anything but play outside, and it sure as hell isn't a school day in early August. The street remains empty, though.

"Maybe it's the weather," she whispers. She hopes that's the case.

The gate squeals on its hinges as she nudges it open. She unsnaps the holster on her service pistol. She doesn't want to pull it, but she refuses to be caught with her pants down.

The smell is stronger here. It reminds her of her childhood, when her mother used to take her to the butcher to get ribs and sausage. It can't be a good sign.

She feels colder as she steps onto the porch. She checks to see if there's more shade there, but the lack of sun makes the difference all but invisible. Maybe it's her nerves.

Calm, Megan.

She knocks on the screen's frame. The metallic sound travels up and down the street, teases her spine.

"LAPD!" she calls. A dying echo answers her.

"Nobody home?" Christian asks.

"Or somebody's hiding." She doesn't think that's the case. Not if some kid went tearing up the street not thirty minutes before their arrival.

The door hangs open a foot or so, probably because the running kid didn't take the time to shut it all the way. She cranes her neck in an attempt at getting a good look inside. The smell punches her in the nose and almost staggers her. The buzzing of flies follows hot on its heels. This isn't the butcher shop; it's something worse.

She searches the shadows with her eyes, and she feels her hand reach for her pistol. There's something dark smeared across the only visible wall in wide streaks that look like they might have been done by hand. She doesn't need her eyes to adjust to know it's blood.

"Christian, call for back up."

She draws her pistol and pulls open the screen.

Rawls rolls his powerful shoulders and then opens the door to interrogation room four. The Gray Street homie they pulled in looks about how he suspected. You bring in a banger for questioning, he plays it one of two ways. He either goes cocky or quiet.

This one's chosen quiet. He sits behind the steel table, wrists cuffed to the rails on either side, and he doesn't move. His heads dips a little as he stares down at the lights reflecting in the tabletop. What Rawls can see of his eyes looks peaceful. There's no anger or anxiety in the man's face, just a flaccid calm, like a toy that needs new batteries. It stands out in contrast with the blood that still coats the man's mouth and jaw, stains his throat and has soaked his gray T-shirt a darker color. If the homie notices, he isn't letting on. Maybe he thinks nobody will see it if he doesn't point it out. Bangers aren't always the smartest kids on the block.

"Hi," Rawls says as he shuts the door behind him. He glances at the camera in the room's upper corner. The closed circuit cable runs down the wall, leaving him one good yank away from complete privacy. Just the way he likes it.

He pulls out a chair and sits down across from the blood-soaked man. "You have a name?"

No answer. The banger sits there like he's in a trance.

"You want to talk about why you and your boy went certifiable this morning?"

Rawls sits and waits. He tries to read the banger's face, but he finds nothing he can pull. Guy's about as close to asleep as a body can be without snoring. Or maybe his mind's just up and gone. Maybe he's realized what he was chewing on back at the Edgar's, and now his brain's gone haywire trying to make some kind of sense of it all.

Or maybe the guy's crashing from whatever drug put him sky high in the first place. Reality's crashing in, and his body and brain are shutting down in order to deal with it.

Rawls rubs a hand over his face as he processes the thoughts and theories. He feels pressure at his temples. It's all fine and dandy if this guy's brain has turned to mush, but he needs to find out if there's some seriously dangerous shit on the streets. If this is a new drug or the start of some serious dick-waving, he needs to know, needs to stomp it down before it gets out of control. He can't let this piece of shit give him the silent treatment.

"Last chance, homie. You want to talk to me, or are you just gonna sit there like a sack of assholes?"

The banger doesn't answer. If he's even heard the words that echo through the tiny room, he gives no sign.

"All right. We'll play it your way." He pushes back his chair and stands. He steps to the wall and wraps his fingers around the cable that travels to the camera's rear. He pulls, and the connection is severed. The cable coils sloppily on the ground.

He turns to face the Gray Streeter, who still refuses to move or even lift his eyes.

"For the record," Rawls says, "I'm going to enjoy the hell out of this."

2Bit nearly rips his mom's screen door off the hinges as he charges into the house. It snaps back to bang against the frame, and his mom's angry voice rips through the run-down home. 2Bit's already in the bathroom, though. He throws the lock a split second before her fists rattle the doorknob.

"Darrel, where you been? You don't slam my doors, you hear me?"

"Shit, Moms! I be out in a minute. Leave me alone!" He hears bravery in his voice, but he sure as hell don't feel it. All he feels is cold and hollow and a growing terror like a feeling he's being chased by something he can't see yet. A dog that sticks to the shadows and growls just loud enough to tell you it's there. It's coming, though. He don't know why, but he's sure that dog's coming.

He examines his hands. There's still some blood on them, though not nearly as much. He wiped most of it off on his T-shirt, ditched the fucking thing in a trashcan four blocks away. He knows it wasn't the smartest move, but his brain tells him he's got other shit to worry about.

He turns the faucet on all the way and starts scrubbing. He works the soap into his hands until his skin aches and stings. He can't seem to get all the blood, though. No matter how hard he scrubs, a few deep trails of the stuff just won't come clean.

"Fuck!"

He balls his hands into fists and brings them down on the sink. Pain travels up his arms to find a home in his spine. He stares at himself in the mirror and tries to make sense of what he sees. Spatters and streaks of blood mark his face, his neck. His eyes are wide and much too white. He stares into them and watches his pupils grow smaller and smaller until they nearly disappear. His lip quivers, and tracks of sweat race each other down his forehead. He looks scared, crazy. He don't recognize this terrified homeboy looking back at him.

Maybe the guy in the mirror is somebody new. Maybe the homeboy he used to be died last night. Maybe that's why he don't remember where he was or what he done.

2Bit clamps his eyes shut tight and watches stars burst behind his eyelids. He presses his fingers to his eyes, and the stars grow brighter. They dance in pulsing fields of green and blue and red. It all looks crazy, like something from a different world.

Then the stars disappear and an image flashes through his brain. He sees himself kicking a gagged and bound Mexican, a Loco, arms covered in ink. The man grunts into his gag, so he kicks him again. He has a knife in his hand. Other Gray Street Bangers stand next to him, blades in their fists. There's laughter. And blood. And somebody starts screaming. Beneath it all he hears a voice, quiet and gentle and a little amazed.

"He stepped through."

2Bit opens his eyes and gasps. He looks at his reflection and almost cries when he sees it pointing at him, smiling.

Ricky keeps shop in a shithole apartment off Rosecrans. Walker knows the dealer can afford better digs, but the building with the central courtyard offers good security. Ricky rents four additional one-rooms, and he keeps soldiers stashed in each. Anybody tries to come in and start shit, they have to climb three flights of stairs with bullets flying at them from four different directions. Going on five years, and Ricky hasn't been knocked over yet.

Walker opens the iron gate and enters the courtyard. He doesn't worry about catching a round. Ricky's boys know he's a friendly. Their boss owes him for more than a couple of in-roads to new markets.

The courtyard bakes with heat despite the overcast skies. The air presses against his skin. It feels wet and hot in his lungs, making breathing a fun little challenge. Maybe the air is the reason he doesn't spot any kids out playing. Usually, the hole is a little more jumping.

He starts up the stairs. His footsteps echo like gunshots through the air. He stomps at the top of the stairwell to get Ricky's attention, and the sound rings out like a shotgun blast. No reply comes. He hears no children or televisions or radios. The building even deflects the sounds of the Compton streets. He wonders if it's always been that way and he just never noticed it. Something tells him it's a new phenomenon. Weird fucking day.

He reaches the top floor without catching a hint of life in the building. Hairs rise on the back of his neck. He wants to draw his pistol or at least unsnap his holster, but he fears giving the soldiers anything that might violate his friendly status.

He keeps his eyes peeled as he reaches Ricky's door. He delivers his knock, three and then two.

"Yeah," comes the reply. Ricky's voice, but a little off. Weak, maybe. "C'mon in."

Walker turns the knob and opens the door.

"Holy shit," Megan says through grit teeth. "Holy fucking shit."

Beside her, Christian begins to cough and gag. She hears him stumble-run back outside and wretch, but she can't peel her eyes off the scene in front of her.

The home's living room is a slaughter pen. Parts of what must be a dozen Mexican men litter the floor. Heads and arms and torsos decorate the room in piles. Sightless eyes stare at ceilings, walls, and discarded flesh. The thick scents of blood and shit fill the room like a fog and force Megan's hand to her mouth and nose. The soapy smell of her palm does next to nothing to improve the air.

She hears Christian coughing again. The sound provides a staccato counterpoint to the constant droning of the flies that fill the living room like a cloud. She hears sirens approaching from far away, and she guesses their backup is on its way.

She tries to make sense of the horrific sight in front of her. The tats covering the discarded arms mark the bodies as members of The Locos. The house is deep in

Gray Street territory. The knowledge does not comfort her, though. This is hell and gone from any gang violence she's seen in her three years on the job. If the Gray Street boys have decided to step up their game, they've done it in the most psychotic way possible.

"Megan!" Christian says as he enters the house again. "Backup's a block away."

"Good," she says. She points at something with her toe, thirteen fleshy objects lined up in a neat row on the blood-sopping carpet. "Are those…"

"Jesus. Tongues."

"This is some serious shit."

"Can you read that?"

Christian points through the swirling mass of flies. The black cloud shifts, and Megan sees writing on the wall. Somebody has covered most of the living room wall with scrawled words. She can't make out much through the shadows. The words are written in a sloppy scrawl, and she can only make out fragments. She tries to make sense of them but fails.

A Darkness Below…and All…Rises.

She makes out the phrase several times among the writing. As the writing approaches the lower right hand corner, it grows more and more erratic, almost desperate. It's a scribble of words she's never seen or heard, never even imagined. It pulls at her, and she takes a step forward before she realizes what she's doing.

"Look," Christian says. His voice startles her back into her head. He points to the opposite wall, and Megan follows with her eyes.

Only three words fill this wall. Somebody wrote them in huge letters, making great sweeps with a blood-soaked hand. They work together with the nonsense words to create a sense of dread deep in Megan's chest. This isn't a gang thing. This is something new and terrible, and it's something she can't mold into any kind of sense.

She reads the words again, and they spread through her mind like ice across a pane of glass.

HE STEPPED THRU

Rawls bounces the banger's head off the steel table. The sound stabs at his ears a few times as it bounces around the tiny space. He expects the homeboy to follow it with some noise of his own: a scream, a grunt. Something. The Gray Streeter keeps quiet, though. Hell, he's silent.

"You wanna talk to me now, you fuck?" He tightens his hand into a fist and slams it into the homeboy's sternum. He hears the man's air rush out in a violent burst, but again the banger doesn't make any sound that would indicate pain.

Fuck it. He's cracked thicker skulls in the past.

"We're running out of chances, shithead. You keep giving me this silent treatment bullshit, and I'm going to have to do some serious damage.

"So what was that bullshit at the restaurant? New drug on the streets? Turf beef? Is this the start of a war? Tell me what we're looking at."

Nothing.

"Fucking answer me!"

The banger looks up at him and smiles. The corners of his mouth creep upward slowly, like an old man climbing stairs. His eyes brim with shadows and fire, and Rawls almost thinks he can see the insanity and desperate anger in them. It's the first time the man has acknowledged his existence, and suddenly he wishes he was anywhere but interrogation room four.

He suppresses a shiver as he eyes the glittering teeth behind blood-caked lips. "Well? You have anything to tell me?"

The banger opens his mouth and speaks in a whispering voice. The unintelligible syllables sound like a broken speaker, all static and air.

Rawls blinks. He tries to say something, but his throat clicks and nothing else comes.

The banger's smile widens.

"Everything and all. There is a darkness below, and it rises."

"What?"

"But he stepped through."

He stares as the banger juts his tongue past his teeth. The wiggling muscle is a dull non-color, and it extends farther than Rawls thinks should be possible, inches becoming a foot.

And then the Gray Street boy bites clean through.

Blood spills from the man's lips like somebody's cranked a faucet. Rawls watches in stunned silence for a moment, trying to figure out just what the fuck he's supposed to do. He thinks of the camera and the cord he yanked free. They'll think he did this. No one will believe him. They put him in here to get the truth, and now a gangbanger is going to bleed to death in an interrogation room while his tongue flops on the table like a dying fish.

He backs against the door and reaches for the knob. He almost turns it, but then he realizes the banger is still smiling. He stares at the dribbling mouth. He hears blood patter onto the tabletop. At the edge of his vision he can see the tongue writhing in a puddle of crimson. He shifts his gaze as the severed muscle rears back like a snake, and the sight gives him the strength he needs to leave the tiny room.

"Help! I need some help up here!"

Walker enters the apartment and closes the door behind him. Out of sight, he finally unsnaps his holster. It comforts him the slightest bit, but he still feels anticipation in his gut like a chunk of ice.

It stinks in Ricky's place, stinks right to hell and back. He's knocked down doors in houses full of dogs that didn't smell this bad. How long has it been since he's seen Ricky?

"Ricky? Where you at?"

Shadows clog the apartment. Shafts of diseased light pierce the cracked blinds, but darkness hides most of the living room. Walker makes out the couch he knows is always there, the coffee table piled high with empty beer cans and bottles. A glass bong sits in the middle of it all. Discarded foil rests nearby. Sloppy.

He reaches for the light switch and flips it on. Nothing. He toggles the switch a few times, and Ricky's weakened voice creeps out of the bedroom.

"Broke the bulbs, man. Watch your step."

Walker does as he's told. Way it smells, he's liable to plop a foot down in a pile of fresh shit. He fishes a lighter out of his pocket and flicks it. A tiny flame pops to life. He adjusts it—letting it grow a little—and he starts forward.

Discarded cans and fast food wrappers fill the floor. He kicks them out of the way, and he hears a squeak as a rat runs from his sweeping foot.

"Jesus Christ."

"Don't think so," comes the answer.

Walker doesn't want to take his time. He wants to leave the apartment just as fast as he can. He needs to talk to Ricky, though. Needs to know what the dealer knows.

He reaches the bedroom door, and a smell like an outhouse slams into him. He brings a hand to his face, and the lighter dies. It doesn't matter, because Ricky has a candle burning on the night stand. It illuminates the dealer's gaunt, naked body, the wild look in his eyes, and the shit-stained bedclothes he's tangled in. Its dancing flame glints off the chromed automatic that lies at its base, reveals the melted stumps of the dozen or so candles that have burned down already, their wax trailing down the front of the night stand like a tumor.

And the candle illuminates the dead girl, too. She's maybe sixteen, maybe a little less. Her wrists are ragged wounds caked with dried blood. One of her arms rests against the wall, just a foot or so below the smeared words.

HE STEPPED THRU

"Hey, Walker," Ricky says. "Jesus don't roll here no more."

2Bit curls into a ball beneath the shower's burning spray and shivers. Flitting memories cut him like blades. Darkness that moves. Blood. Knives doing horrible things.

45

Strange words.

Writing with his bloody palm.

2Bit cries.

Megan stands outside the house, at the end of the broken walk. She stares at the empty street while the assigned detective combs through the pile of bodies in the living room. She doesn't know why she's out here. It's not fair. Detective Bagley told her to keep the scene clear, but the street remains empty. Only squad cars line the curb. And she gets to guard them. Bullshit.

She thinks about the words. *He stepped thru. A Darkness Below.* What do they mean? She knows it all fits together somehow, and she knows with every last bit of her brain that she can figure it out if they'd just let her look at them some more.

"You okay?" Christian asks. He's regained some of his color and doesn't look so much like bad cheese anymore.

"Fine."

"You sure? That was some freaky shit."

"I'm fine. Pinky swear, okay?" She gives him a glare so he'll get the fucking picture.

"All right."

She turns her eyes back to the street, but in the back of her mind she still sees the words.

He stepped thru.

"Ricky? What the fuck, man?"

"Walker. Always good to see a slice I know."

"Jesus Christ. What the hell is going on here? I sure as fuck hope you don't expect me to clean this mess up for you."

"What mess?" Ricky looks around in a daze. Walker watches his eyes bounce around the room, lost. Finally, the dealer catches a glimpse of the dead girl beside him and the shit they're both lying in. "Oh, that. That's a real bitch of a story, Walker man."

"Why don't you tell it?"

"Don't think I should. You won't like the ending much."

Walker feels the first fingers of anger tickle his spine. The prick's trying to play him, string him along for some unknown reason.

"Don't give me that shit, Ricky. How many streets have I opened up for you? How many times have I steered the department in a different direction so you could keep operating? You fucking owe me."

Ricky stares into space for a long moment, and Walker can see the rusty gears turning in the man's head. He wonders if this will be the moment when Ricky's mind breaks. Maybe everything will crash in on the dealer's brain and shatter it like porcelain.

"Fine," Ricky says. His voice rings with surrender. "Was Dobbs got the whole thing rolling."

"So Dobbs is still in charge? This isn't some new guy proving he's got cajones?"

"Naw. All this shit is Dobbs. That nigga gonna run the world."

"What's going on, Ricky? Get to the heart of it, okay?"

"So the big man says he got something new, says he

found religion and shit. Says it's gonna put Gray Street back on top of things. A lotta niggas was snickering about that shit. What? We gonna go preach our corners back from the Locos and Niners? Fuck that shit, man. These niggas wanna come correct, wanna roll up on a muthafucka and take they shit back. They don't wanna be using God or some shit to do they dirty work.

"So Dobbs calls a meet couple weeks back, gets the whole fucking tribe together. Pulls everybody into a warehouse, and suddenly I'm surrounded by niggas I ain't seen in ages, folks I didn't know was even in the life no more.

"We all standing around for a while, and then Dobbs comes in with this book. It's one of those big fucking leather jobs, but it don't look like leather. It looks like some nigga's skin was used on it. That can't be right, though. Least I thought so then."

Ricky takes the dead girl's hand in his own. Walker wants to look away but finds he can't. He watches as Ricky places the corpse's finger in his mouth and sucks.

"Ricky."

The dealer lets the hand drop. "Yeah?"

"Keep talking."

"Right. So Dobbs talks about this book he found, how it's full of secrets and dark shit, talking about other worlds and things humans ain't supposed to know. 'There's something out there,' he says. 'A darkness below. Everything and all.' He reads from it, and it weren't in no language I ever heard before. Weird thing is, I could *feel* those words. It was like they crawled through the room and grabbed me. I could feel they fingers wrapping around my heart, and suddenly I just wanted to kill something. I could see it in them other gangstas eyes, too. Everybody in that place was going crazy. One nigga beat down the homeboy standing next to him, just knocked him to the floor and started stomping until the nigga's head split open."

"Nobody did anything?"

"Plenty of niggas did stuff, Walker. I watched one homeboy jerk off while the shit was going down. Another waited for homeboy's skull to crack, and then he grabbed a handful of brains and started eating. Yeah, folks was doing all kinds of stuff."

"Holy shit."

"Nothing holy about it, man. Nothing at all."

"You sure it's not a drug, Ricky? Maybe he pumped the air full of shit. Hell, I don't know."

"Drugs wear off, man. These niggas been getting crazier and crazier. See, when Dobbs was talking all this shit about other worlds and shit, these homeboys got to talking about going there, about sending somebody to check it all out."

"Sending Dobbs, you mean."

"Give the cracka a prize."

"You can't be serious."

Ricky chuckles, a cold sound like stones colliding. His chest jumps a little. "What you see today, got you in my place? See some weird shit? You asking 'bout some nigga flashing his balls around, something bad musta jumped up. What you see, Walker man?"

He shakes his head. He doesn't want to talk about the giggler or his little hobby. He sure as hell doesn't want to talk about the homeboy eating a little boy's heart.

"What I thought," Ricky says. "I know you, man. You one of them muthafuckas likes to talk. You clam up like this, you musta seen some new shit. Probably witness something you don't think us gangstas was capable of. I right?"

"Maybe."

"What I thought. Shit done got deep, Walker. Get a shovel, man. Ain't nothing to do now but dig."

"That what you think?"

"Shit jumpin' off, it means they did it. They put Dobbs through."

"There was a plan? Tell me about it."

"They was gonna do it last night. Heard some niggas saying they had to 'Weaken the walls' or some shit. Said they'd snatched a bunch of Locos for a sacrifice. You believe that shit? Goddamn sacrifice. That shit's crazy, right? I want to think so, but I been seeing things since that meet. Shit you wouldn't believe, man. You ask me, I think the walls already be weak. I think Dobbs just needed a push."

"Fuck."

"Yeah."

"He stepped through. So that's what it means? They believed this shit enough they were gonna try."

"Looks like, homie. Looks like they pulled that shit off, too."

Walker feels the ice spread through his system. He refuses to believe the shit Ricky's trying to spoon-feed him. "Where's Dobbs going to be now?"

"Who knows? Might not even be in this world no more, right?"

"Let's say he's in the here and now. Where would I find him?"

"Safe house off Rose."

"I know the one. How many guards?"

"One or two at most."

"You're joking."

"Shit, Walker. Dobbs don't need guards no more."

"That was before he started fucking up my town."

"Right."

Ricky's head droops, his chin meeting his chest. He sits that way for a long time, and Walker thinks maybe the dealer's passed out. He should get out of the apartment. He's getting used to the smells of shit and blood and decay, and that can't be a good sign.

He turns to leave, and Ricky jumps in the bed.

"Hey, Walker?"

"Yeah."

"The sun come out today?"

"No."

"What I thought." Ricky snatches the gleaming pistol off the nightstand. Walker steps forward, but the dealer already has the barrel under his chin. The man's eyes are haunted but somehow calm.

"It rises."

Ricky pulls the trigger, and what's left of his mind paints the ceiling.

EVENING

Walker stands beside Rawls in a dark corner of the motor pool. He looks into his partner's eyes and sees lingering traces of fear. He figures Rawls sees the same in him.

"They took the guy to Mercy, but he died in transport. Just bled out."

"Jesus."

"The tongue was the worst part. Fucking thing kept moving for almost a half hour."

"Ricky's wasn't a pretty scene, either."

"And Thomas still isn't gonna work on getting us a warrant."

"Bullshit."

"I mean, I see it. We don't have any direct ties to this shit, but still."

Walker rubs his face with hands that need to be washed. It's been too long a day, and he knows it isn't near done. "It's got to stop though, man. This fuck pile we saw today is only gonna get worse if gangbangers are on the streets trying to go voodoo on us."

Rawls nods.

"But if we take down Dobbs tonight, it could stop. Somebody with a good head on their shoulders moves up, and the streets go quiet again."

"Who moves up?" Rawls asks.

"Whoever we back. That doesn't matter until tomorrow."

Rawls stares at the pavement for a long moment. Thoughts cross his face as creases of worry. His breath is a slow, purring thing.

Finally, he looks up.

"Great. Let's grease this asshole."

Megan lifts the yellow crime scene tape and enters the house for the second time. The dead Mexicans are gone, carted off to the county hospital and deposited in the morgue, but no one has come to clean the scene yet. That's good.

With night coming on fast, darkness saturates the house. She sees faint shapes, but no details. She steps onto the soaked carpet and hears it squelch beneath her shoes. The scents of death remain. She breathes deep and feels the aroma creep through her body, latch onto her bones and work its way into her very structure.

She clicks on the flashlight in her hand and aims it at the wall. The words scroll from ceiling to floor. They've dried a little more, and now they're a dark brown against the yellowed paint.

Why am I here? she wonders. *Why on earth am I doing this?*

Because you want to.

She begins to read.

"We are everything and, and we are one and the same...."

Walker pulls onto Rose and slows the car a little. They're three blocks away from Dobbs' safe house, and he feels insects crawling through his belly. He thinks about one banger playing games with a girl's intestines and another eating a child's heart. He thinks about the empty apartment building and the dead girl in Ricky's bed, the look of quiet horror in the dealer's eyes in the second before he pulled the trigger. He thinks about all of it, and he wonders what might be waiting for them three blocks down the street.

"You ready for this?" he asks Rawls.

"Sure thing."

He takes his eyes from the road and gives his partner a look. "I'm serious. Are you ready for this?"

A shrug. "I think so. Shit, I don't know. What are we gonna see at this place? What's Dobbs gonna be up to?"

"I wish I knew."

"I wish I didn't have to find out."

"Amen."

"I'm not gonna lie, man. The shit we've seen today, it's got me spooked pretty bad."

"Me too."

"Yeah?"

"Swear. Look, there's the majority of my brain. It says this is just a bunch of strung-out gangbangers talking out their asses and acting crazy because they got a bad cut of dust or something."

"But?"

"But then there's the part of my head that saw the look in those bangers' eyes. They believed this shit, I mean really believed it. I think about that—about the sheer *belief* I saw in their faces—and it gets me thinking."

"I know what you mean."

"I know you do."

He hears Rawls take a deep breath. The man lets it out slow. "So what do you want to do?"

"I want us to be careful. You watch my back, and I'll watch yours. Same deal as always."

Rawls nods. "Deal."

"Okay." He pulls the car over to the curb and yanks the ski mask down over his face. "Time to go to work."

2Bit doesn't want to go back in the house. He wants to run away. He wants to hurt himself, put a gun to his head and pull the trigger, blast any more memories all to hell. He can't do it, though. His legs keep pulling him toward the house.

He remembers what he put in the pot on the stove. He remembers cutting them off the dead Mexicans one at a time. Normal homeboys don't do that shit. Crazy motherfuckers do.

He don't want to be crazy.

But his legs won't stop dragging him forward.

He sees the yellow tape criss-crossing the open door. He thinks the door should be shut, but then he sees the light inside, a single beam that roams back and forth, pointing at the living room wall. He sees images of himself dipping his finger in a shallow puddle of blood and writing letters on the wall. He grinds his teeth, closes his eyes, and the images disappear.

It could be a cop in the house. He knows it's dangerous, but his legs just keep moving. Somewhere in his mind, he knows he's lost control. The house has him now. The things he did there changed him, and it doesn't matter if he remembers all of them or not. Now, he's playing a part. He wants desperately to break free, but he fails again and again.

He grabs the yellow tape in both hands and rips it down. The flashlight's beam moves, finds his face. The white spot blinds him, but he don't blink.

"Hi," a voice says. Female. Deep. The light returns to the wall, and somehow he can see her. She's tall, pale. She stands naked in the middle of the blood-drenched room. He sees a uniform discarded at her feet. Five-oh. He watches as she shifts her weight and old blood smears her toes. He hears her voice repeat words he barely remembers writing. He turns and follows the flashlight as it roams words he'd never imagined before last night.

"I wrote those," he says.

"I know. They're beautiful."

He approaches and stands at her side. He places a hand on the small of her back and feels sweat on her smooth skin.

"Why you here?" he asks. He hears his voice shake, and he realizes his body is burning with anticipation.

"For you," she whispers.

She drops the flashlight, and her arms close around him.

* * *

Walker rushes down the sidewalk in a crouch. His service pistol feels warm in his hands. He hears Rawls' nearly-silent footsteps right behind him.

Rose Street is quiet, dark. No voices or music or television programs. No cats yowling into the night or dogs barking at yowling cats. Something has turned Compton into a ghost town.

He reaches the gate that leads to Dobbs' safe house. He remembers the last time he was here, delivering a witness to some of the Gray Street rank and file. He kept a lid on a war with that delivery. He hopes his presence here tonight will do something similar. He reaches out to open the front gate and realizes he doesn't have to.

Rawls taps him on the shoulder, points to the home's front door.

"Shit."

It's standing open, yellow light spilling into the night. From his spot on the sidewalk he can see the legs sprawled in the opening. It reminds him of the kid with a hole in his torso.

Something awful has already happened here.

Walker motions for Rawls to follow. "C'mon!"

Together they rush toward the front door.

Waves of pleasure surge through Megan's body. She bucks on top of the stranger, grinding her hips harder and harder against his. She digs furrows in his chest with her nails. Her breath hitches in her throat, and sweat traces cooling trickles down her body.

Something rumbles deeper in the house, a sound like an angry lion stalking prey through high grasses.

A spike of ecstasy pierces her spine, and she cries out. The man beneath her grunts in a steady rhythm.

"We are everything and all," she says between panting breaths. She can sense the blood that soaks the carpet creep toward their heat. It's almost time. She's never felt more alive. More needed.

"Darkness below!" she gasps.

"He stepped through," the man says.

The rumble becomes a roar.

The yellow light pulses as Walker crosses the threshold. He recoils from the body in the doorway. Basketball shoes and baggy track pants give way to a torso that's been skinned. Bloody muscle catches the sick light and spins it off in different directions. The corpse lacks a head, and Walker wonders if they'll find it in the house.

"Mother of all hell," Rawls whispers as they enter the living room. Half a dozen corpses line the room. Somebody's nailed their wrists and throats to the walls. They stand in a mockery of life, their faces glazed with something that's both wonder and horror. A woman whose legs have been torn away wears her dying scream like a mask. The bare spaces that remain between the bodies have been filled with writing.

"Fuck," Rawls says. "That's the sort of shit that banger spouted in interrogation."

"Quiet."

Walker watches the bodies. Dobbs isn't one of them. He imagines them tearing loose from the wall and shambling toward him. He shakes the thought away. Until he finds Dobbs, he needs to concentrate.

Another light pulses from the kitchen doorway. It cycles faster than the living room's bulb, almost quick enough to be a strobe light. It matches the speed of his racing heartbeat. He feels it pull him like a strange, false gravity.

He catches Rawls' eye and then cocks his head at the doorway. His partner nods.

Walker steps into the kitchen, his pistol up and his trigger finger itching.

A muscular, naked man stands at the sink, facing away from them. The flesh of his back ripples as he breathes in and out. Blood smears his skin. More coats the cracked linoleum.

"Malcolm Dobbs," Walker says. "Turn around nice and fucking slow."

The man's skin ripples again. Walker sees something that looks like a thick cord wriggle beneath the flesh. He blinks, and it disappears.

"You ever wonder what's behind the world?" the man asks. He starts to turn around.

"Hands up!" Walker orders. "Behind your head, asshole."

The man keeps talking as he follows Walker's command. "I used to wonder all the time, used to really want to learn that shit." His voice sounds strange. Maybe wet. "I knew this wasn't all there was, man. There had to be something else, something below. A darkness."

Malcolm Dobbs smiles. Blood runs from the corners of his mouth, from his nose and ears and eyes. Something rips.

Walker thinks it's too hot in the kitchen. The air closes in on him. Somewhere far away, he hears somebody blubber. Maybe Rawls. Who knows?

"I opened a door in the wall," Dobbs says. He coughs once, and a wet morsel splats against the floor. "And I stepped through."

Walker senses Rawls falling to his knees. He feels tears sting at his eyes. "You're under arrest," he says, but the words leave his mouth as a croaking sob. He knows he should pull the trigger, but he can't find the strength. He can barely stand.

"The door doesn't close, though. It just hangs open. I tried, but I can't budge the motherfucker."

The light strobes faster and faster. Walker sees fingers claw at the inside of Dobbs' body, fighting to break free. He feels his mouth fall open. A sound comes out, and he thinks he might be screaming.

Dobbs' smile splits at the corners. Holes appear in his chest.

Walker shoves the pistol in his hand past his lips to cut off the scream.

Darkness.

SOMETHING
WENT
WRONG

When Thomas heard the first knock at the motel room door, he chose to ignore it. Instead, he focused on the dust. Lots of dust. Everywhere he looked. It spiraled in streaks on the fake brass doorknob, and it coated the chipped nightstand in a thin sheet. Motes twirled lazy pirouettes through the shafts of hot sunlight that chopped the room from window to wall. With a grim set to his mouth, he decided he hated the room. Of all the places to meet.

A groan from the bathroom. He ignored that, too.

He tugged the handkerchief from his back pocket and blew his nose into it. All the dust was going to turn his allergies into a real trial. Cedar season only made matters worse. January in Austin, Texas. Already, it appeared 1958 was going to be an awful year.

Another knock. Not urgent, but with a little more authority than the first. His eyes ticked to the door, the pool of shadow that filled that corner of the room. He'd have to cross the floor to reach it.

So what? He found no need to keep stalling, so he climbed to his feet and brushed his hands down the front of his slacks. With steps both lazy and staccato, he crossed the room, slicing his way through the space, thinking about the dust crashing across his chest and feeling his sinuses grow angry, the pressure there inching toward awful. As he reached for the doorknob, another groan drifted from behind the closed bathroom door. He cast a single sneer toward the room as the sound died. So much trouble. All the damn trouble in the whole damn world.

He rubbed his fingertips together, the sound like sandpaper, and then turned the knob. The latch clicked, and he pulled open the door. Orange light fell on him, and he squinted. Something shuffled outside the door, and he gave his guest a pained smile, motioned to enter while still trying to shield his eyes.

Heavy footsteps passed him, maybe not footsteps but stones being dropped at regular intervals. He recognized old shoes on cheap floors when he heard them, though. When he heard the creek of rusty bedsprings and knew the visitor was past him, he closed the door and waited for his sight to return, standing there with his hands crossed behind his back.

When his sight returned, he saw the white, wrinkled shirt with the top button undone, the dry waddle of throat that rested in that V of fabric. He saw eyes that were gray and wide and a little shiny with water, saw the calm and cold determination. And the thrill. The old man had eyes like a clever and mean child, capable of thrusting knives with a wink.

The old man—the name Jenkins didn't quite fit—watched him, sitting on the edge of the bed and saying nothing. Fingertips drummed on cotton trousers. Feet in scuffed shoes ground into the floor and then fell still. A swallow filled the silence like the twisting of a stretched rope.

Thomas watched Jenkins and refused to show any emotion. He resisted itches and breathed deep, ignoring the dust that tickled his nose and throat. Through moments that stretched and refused to yield, he held still and kept his eyes on those gray irises. Moments became minutes, became longer.

Jenkins breathed deep and released a disappointed sigh. He clapped his hands against his knees and hitched his shoulders into a shrug.

"Well?"

He shook his head and rubbed his temples. "Something went wrong."

"Then steps must be taken."

"Like?"

The old man's eyes shifted to the side. For a brief moment, his fingers resumed their cadence. Then, he swallowed again before examining his nails.

"Tell me who knows."

The first sack arrives after midnight.

Ben wakes when somebody pounds on the door. The hammering sound startles him from sleep, and he leaps from his bed, his mind already racing. Fire. Tornado. He wonders what other disasters might have occurred, but then he looks out his bedroom window and sees nothing but the apartment complex and a calm night.

He tosses the pillow he had been hugging to his chest. In his dream, it was a woman, somebody warm and wonderful. That was last year, though. Now, it's 2012, and he lives alone. The pillow isn't anybody. Certainly not....

Melissa. Her name appears as his next thought, and he rushes from the room in T-shirt and boxers, the frantic motion chasing his cat, Simon, under the bed to hide. As he sprints to the door, he thinks of all the things that may have happened. They flash through his brain in a terrible slideshow of car accidents and falls and broken bones. He wonders if maybe something happened to the dogs.

Even so close to frantic, he still checks the peephole. A part of him hopes he'll see Melissa waiting for him. Maybe something's wrong, or maybe she's lonely. He sees nothing but the empty landing outside his apartment though, and it doesn't make any sense. Ideas wander through his head—a drunk or kids playing pranks—but he opens the door, regardless. He's out of bed, and it's almost two in the morning. Might as well go a little farther.

The landing is still. Whoever knocked on his door is long gone. It occurs to him that he didn't hear any footsteps pounding away from the door, but he was mostly asleep at the time. Hell, he still is. As he leans his head out and looks left and right, the world sits behind a haze of fatigue, all the edges soft, the distances different than they should be.

He almost fails to notice the sack. Grumbling, he starts to close the door, but his eyes catch sight of crinkled brown paper. Pausing, his head sticking out from behind the door like a snooping old woman, he eyes the bag. A simple, paper lunch sack, the top rolled shut. It sits there like a lonely puppy, almost expectant. He sniffs at the air, but doesn't smell anything. The suspicion it might contain a nice lump of shit weighs in his mind, but then maybe the bag would be on fire. He remembers the prank well. His step-father used to tell him about it whenever he tried to be funny.

Cautiously, Ben steps out from behind the door and lowers himself into a crouch. He reaches for the bag. The paper feels old and soft against his fingers, and his eyebrows knit with curiosity as he unrolls the sack and opens it, tilting it so he can peer inside.

He gasps and almost throws the sack across the hall. Instead, he recoils, something hitching hard in his throat. Scrambling backward, he slams the door and locks it before dashing for his cell phone. His fingers are numb and shaking, and it takes him three tries to dial 911.

The phone rings once, and an operator appears, her voice calm, almost bored. He tells her his name and address, and he tells her what was in the sack. She says a police officer is on the way, and he screams when something brushes his ankle. The operator asks if he's in danger, and embarrassment burns in his voice as he tells her he's fine, that he'll wait for the police.

He hangs up the phone and reaches down to scratch the scruff of Simon's chin. The cat wants to be fed.

"Okay, for serious. What is it?"

Jim slapped a flashlight into her hand. He clicked his on with the press of a button. "You're not gonna believe it."

"When I don't even know what it is? How can I?"

"Just come on. It's awesome."

Rose gave Jim a look that told him it better be more than amazing. Whatever he had to show her had better change her life. It had best shoot right past amazing and become amaze-balls. She'd only left her apartment and come to the restaurant because she thought she'd have to talk her boss out of burning it down. Now, he wanted to show her something?

She followed as Jim led her out of Jimmy's Party Harbor and across the parking lot toward the docks. Her boss almost had a skip to his step, and she wondered what could possibly have him so excited. By the time he waved for her to follow and started down the concrete ramp toward the boat slips, she'd decided he'd scored some coke again and was convinced that this time she really would fuck him. Stifling a groan, she rolled her right shoulder. Best to get the hook warmed up now. Last time she'd punched him, the arm had spent two weeks in a sling.

"Jim, you know you get coke dick something fierce. Don't make me slug you when you can't even get it up."

"You wish, my darling."

He reached the first of the wooden docks and hopped onto it. A hollow noise rang through the valley. If he was hoping to nail her, he was searching in the wrong place for a hump-and-pump spot. Once or twice before, he'd tried to get her on one of the boats, but 2011 had been a brutal year. With eight months of clear, hot skies stretched out behind it, Lake Travis had reached new lows. Four of the restaurant's five docks now rested on dry and cracked lakebed. What water surrounded the fifth was so shallow, few dared get close enough to consider using it.

Rose paused at the end of the ramp. Beneath the stars and half moon, it appeared woefully depressing. Looking out at the beached docks, the cracked ground, she thought she'd never seen the lake this low, that it must have dropped a few more feet over night. She felt bad for Jim. The restaurant had been a great idea a few years back, a place you could drive or boat to, with great music and strong drinks. As recently as last year, Lake Travis had constantly been hopping, with good water bringing families out for a day in the sun and the drunk assholes coming in from Devil's Cove. Now, those days were relics, gone the way of her food costs and the restaurant's profit margin.

"Move your ass!" Jim was at the far end of the dock, flapping his arms overhead, the beam from his flashlight leaping all over.

"You promise you're not just trying to fuck me?"

"What?"

"Promise me!"

"Fine, I promise! Not even a handjob!"

"Such a gentleman," she muttered as she clumped her way down the dock, her boots like sledgehammers against the old wood. Jim waited for her with a child's grin on his face, bouncing on the balls of his feet. "Are you about to break out a pee-pee dance?"

"Be nice. Earlier, I was up thinking, and I thought I saw something. The lake's gone down some more."

"I noticed. Shit."

"Okay, yeah. It sucks and stuff. Anyway, I came down here to see what's what, and I was right. I totally saw something."

"Good for you?"

"Just come check it out," he said

"If I do it, will you let me go home? I need sleep if I'm gonna keep those stoned assholes doing their prep romorrow."

"You know I will. Now, c'mon!"

Rose rolled her eyes and followed her boss. With the excited twinkle in his eye, he looked less like an authority figure than ever. Curly blond hair, black-rimmed glasses, and two day's worth of stubble marked his face, while the short sleeves of his work shirt barely covered any of the koi, lilies, and other images inked into his arms. Even in the middle of the night, he wore flip-flops.

She followed him to the end of the beached dock and down the iron rungs that had been sunk into its side. A small drop put her on the lakebed. She turned and saw the beam of Jim's flashlight already trailing into the darkness. As carefully as she could, she caught up and fell in step beside him.

"Is it amaze-balls?" she asked.

In the darkness, he gave her a wink and then nodded toward the end of his flashlight's beam. "You tell me."

Rose took a few steps forward, adding her own light to Jim's. She squinted, wondering if the thing in front of her was real or some trick of her imagination. Another step, and she knew.

She turned to Jim. "Holy shit."

* * *

Jenkins sat with his legs crossed, the yellow notepad resting on his knee. He finished writing the fourth name, his pencil sounding dry and violent against the paper, and then he looked up. "Is that all?"

"Yes."

"You're sure?"

"You think I wouldn't be sure?" Thomas thought his voice sounded harsh, almost desperate to his ears. For an instant, he wondered if the man noticed. Then, he decided the question was idiotic. Of course, he'd noticed. He noticed everything.

"Sometimes people forget things. Details..." Jenkins rubbed the pads of his fingers together and then opened them. Dust scattered.

Still so much dust in the room. Another groan came from the bathroom, and he cringed.

"Do you want me to...?" He jerked a thumb toward the bathroom door.

"We have time. Let's focus on this part, first."

"Sure." He would never think to question the old man.

"Do you think they might try to leave the area?"

"What?"

"We need to be concerned with containment, right now," Jenkins said. "We don't want this to spread."

Thomas nodded. A quick flush of shame heated him. "No. There's no reason to think they might leave the area."

"You're positive?"

"Yes."

The old man pursed his lips and nodded. He appeared to be deep in thought, and Thomas wondered what terrible things had to travel through that mind.

Something moved at the edge of his vision. Thomas glanced to the carpet and saw a line of ants marching toward one of the man's scuffed black shoes. He looked at his own shoes to make sure none were near him, and then he looked to Jenkins again.

He was checking his watch. "Well, if they're not going anywhere, there's no reason we can't get some shuteye. I'll take the chair."

The cell fills his hand, and Ben stares at it as he tries to decide what to do. He wants to call, to make sure she's okay, but it's half-past two and heading toward three. For a brief second, he considers driving past the house. It's only five minutes away, maybe less. The police are on the way though, and it isn't as though a drive-by will tell him anything.

Fuck it.

He punches in her name and hits the talk button. Pressing the phone to his ear, he squeezes his eyes shut and pretends her anger won't be too awful. The phone rings five times, six, and then she answers, her voice groggy and cold.

"What the hell?"

For a second, all he can do is breathe. He's so relieved to hear her voice, he forgets his words.

"Ben?"

"Sorry. I, uh…bad dream. I was worried."

"Really?"

"Yeah. It was really vivid, I guess."

"What was it?" she asks.

"Well...."

"Look, just tell me tomorrow. I'm going back to bed."

"Yeah, it doesn't matter. I'm sorry I woke you. Glad you're okay."

"Yeah, sure. Bye."

The phone goes dead, and a sigh pours out of him. Looking at the cell in his hand, he thinks about the pinched look that must have filled Melissa's face. She always looks that way when she's annoyed, and fatigue just makes it worse.

Suddenly, his eyes feel hot. He shoves at the thought, trying to cast it out, and focuses on something positive. At least she isn't hurt. Now, he only has a few dozen questions left. Even if they're terrible questions, at least he knows Melissa is safe.

He glances at the kitchen doorway and sees Simon eating by the fridge, his tail swishing joyfully. "Somebody's gotta be happy," he mutters.

Again, he finds himself approaching the door. His hands flat against its surface, he presses his eye to the peep hole once more and looks across the hall. The sack rests against his neighbor's door. He wonders if maybe he should bring it inside so an animal won't wander off with it, but touching it is the last thing he wants. In his head, he can still see the bloody teeth, how they sat like tiny eggs in a nest of hair the same color as Melissa's. Who would do something like that?

He's still wondering when the police knock on his door five minutes later.

* * *

"You're shitting me."

"I shit you not." Jim's voice buzzed with excitement. Even it he hadn't bumped, he sounded coked up.

Rose dropped into a crouch. With both hands, she brushed her dark curls behind her ears. Then, she trained her flashlight on the thing in front of her and tried to make some kind of sense out of it.

It was a skeleton. Any fool could see that. In a way, it even made sense. With the receding waters uncovering more and more of the past, strange things were bound to turn up. Already, folks had discovered several forgotten peasant villages and a stolen car that had been missing since the eighties. This was different, though. The thing in front of her was a human skeleton, contorted in agony. Chains and weights had been wrapped around it, the tattered remains of a canvas sack clinging here and there. And somebody had shoved a stone in its mouth. That was the detail that really got Rose's heart thumping.

"Why would anybody do that?"

Jim shuffled beside her. "Fuck if I know. Superstition? People are crazy? Shit is nuts?"

"But this is insane. Whoever did this had a lot more than a grudge against this guy."

"Maybe grudges went a lot farther back then?"

"I'm not sure this area was settled during the Dark Ages."

"You know that for sure?"

With narrowed eyes, she looked at Jim, trying to pick his features out of the darkness. "Are you serious right now?"

"About what?"

She pointed at the skeleton. "What do you think, Jim? What are you going to do with that? Why are you calling me instead of the police or something?"

"Why would I call the police?"

"Because somebody shoved a rock in some poor fuck's mouth and dumped him in the lake!"

"Not recently! Shit, not for years! Something like this, it's got to be decades old at the least."

For several seconds, all she could do was blink. Was he serious? "What does it matter? You don't get to just guess at the statute of limitations. You have to report a body if you find it."

Jim shrugged and stepped past her, crouching directly over the splayed skeleton. "Whatever," he said. "On a certain level, right, it's just cool?"

"You are coked up, aren't you?"

A string of giggles poured out of him. "Not going to be able to afford it forever. Might as well, right?"

"Jesus. This isn't some powder joke, is it?"

"What? No!" He looked like he'd been slapped. "I didn't plant this shit. I just found it."

"No. Whatever." She stood there, looking from her boss to the skeleton and back again. Shit, it was just too much.

"You didn't notice the teeth?" Jim asked. He looked a little disappointed.

"I was a little more concerned by the rock just behind them."

"You should look again."

She rolled her eyes and then turned back to the skeleton, leaning in to get a good look as she shone her light on the skull. Her stomach dropped, and her breath stuck in her throat like a rusted fish hook. The skull's canines were far too long, easily double the size of normal teeth. Holy shit, the thing had fangs.

"Interesting, right?" Jim asked.

"Do you have any coke left, or did you do it all?"

He nodded. His expression made him look like a happy puppy. "There's some left."

"Good. Let's go have a little. I can't handle this sort of thing straight."

Thomas woke with a start when something knocked hard on the door. For one terrifying moment, he lay propped up on his elbows, eyes wide and staring as he tried to locate the threat. Had he really fallen asleep with the old man in the room? How could he be so stupid?

Then, another muffled groan drifted from behind the bathroom door, and he realized the kick must have been what he'd stashed there. Sighing, he swung his legs over the side of the bed and sat up. He still wore his clothes, the old pants looking almost as wrinkled as Jenkins. The scuffed shoes kept his feet warm against the morning air. Was it still morning?

He looked around, swiveling his stiff neck, and realized the old man had left the room. Another sigh rattled out him, and this one sounded much more annoyed than the first. Great, so now he had to track down Jenkins on top of everything else. Already, he was exhausted. Sooner or later, the old man would be the death of him. Thomas could only hope he hadn't started on the list. He still prayed he could talk his superior out of what was coming. It was a fool's hope—he knew that—but the years had showed him stranger miracles.

He stood and walked to the table that filled one corner of the hotel room, trying to ignore the pain in his sinuses. His suit jacket waited on the back of one chair, and the .45 waited in his shoulder holster on the back of the other. Joints creaked as he worked the holster on and then covered it with the jacket. Once everything was in place, he rolled his shoulders and felt the ache ease just a little. Okay, he could move.

Before leaving the room, he stepped into the bathroom and checked all the chains. Everything remained tight and secure. The flesh beneath the metal was pink, but it hadn't turned raw and bleeding yet. That was good. He muttered a warning and shut the door behind him. Then, he went to find the old man.

As he walked across the gravel lot, he breathed deep. The morning tasted like dew and old motor oil, perfectly matching the pale yellow and dreary gray of the morning light. Beneath it all, he thought he could already smell cedar. Wonderful.

Everything remained still, the crunch of his footsteps the only sound. He reached the middle of the lot and froze, realizing he didn't know exactly where he was headed. The old man was a peculiar personality, to say the least. Following his particular brand of strangeness could be difficult.

Seeing the diner made it easier, though. Thomas remembered the squat little building full of windows and dirty chrome. A neon sign blinked out of time, and when he listened he could almost hear the sign buzzing. Three cars and a pickup in various states of distress sat in the parking lot. Thomas looked closely, examining the windows for any sign of life. Sure enough, Jenkins sat in a window booth, sipping from a ceramic mug.

His third sigh drifted into the morning air as he started across the street. With each step, he whispered a little prayer that he wouldn't find anything too terrible in the diner, but he didn't think anyone was listening.

He forgets the cop's name. Once or twice, he wants to call the man Detective Edwards, but he's not sure that's right. Instead of risking it, he stays silent and sips his coffee and waits for somebody to talk to him. Already, the detective has spent an hour questioning him, asking if he has any enemies or he can think of anybody who might have pulled a prank. He asks the same questions again and again, as if trying to catch him in a lie, but Ben just answers the same way every time because it's the only way he knows.

Other bodies move through his apartment. Technicians and others in uniforms. The one who probably isn't Detective Edwards weaves his way through them in a manner that suggests he's a little excited. Why shouldn't he be? This is probably a nice change from the typical shootings or stabbings or whatever else police investigate in a mid-size city. Occasionally, the detective stops to chat with his partner, a thin man with a face that looks like it's been carved out of white marble.

The first pale rays of sunlight creep through the window, and Ben remembers how long he's been awake. Soon, he'll need to be at work, but he doesn't think he'll make it in today. If he does call in, he'll have to let Melissa know. She'll be worried if she emails for their morning water run and he doesn't answer, especially after calling her.

Probably Isn't Detective Edwards walks over and says they're almost done, that they think they might have pulled some prints and will run tests on the bag and its contents. Ben sees the items in his head, but he's too exhausted to shudder, so he just nods and thanks the detective, who presses a card into his hand and tells him to call with any questions. He looks at the card and sees he had the name right after all. Yay for him.

Soon, the police leave, and the apartment is empty and quiet. Simon hops onto the couch and curls into a ball. He reaches out and strokes the cat, and then he decides he needs a drink.

Shambling into the kitchen, he wonders if he's moving so slowly because he's tired or because he's sad. He decides it's probably a little of both, with a dash of creeped-the-fuck-out thrown in for flavor. Why else would he pull the bottle of vodka from his freezer at six in the morning? The cold liquor slices its way down his throat, dragging a cough and a shiver from him. He pulls again, and the second hit is a little softer. Not much, but he makes it through with only an ugly sneer to mark its passage.

As a nice wave of heat travels from his gut to the rest of his body, he twists the cap back into place and shoves the bottle back in the freezer. A few deep breaths, and he almost feels normal. Fuck it. Time to go to work.

Rose giggled and clamped her hands around Jim's throat. His face went red, but his smile was playful, even eager. Her laughter turned into a growl as she darted forward and mashed her lips to his. Their mouths opened, and she slid her dry tongue over his, the cocaine leaving their mouths electric and tingling. She loved the sandpaper kisses. Of the many coke effects she enjoyed, it was her favorite by far.

Jim's hand found her hair and tightened into a fist, pulling a pleased sigh from her. The pain ran through her in a hot rush, waking up every inch of her. Pulling away, she gave him a smile before cracking her hand across his face.

Then she released him and stepped away.

"Thanks, boss. That was fun."

Jim looked at her with a shocked expression, like she'd just told him she liked killing senior citizens or something.

"What?" she asked.

"I'm not done," he said

"Done?"

"You know."

"Wait a sec," Rose said. She could barely contain her laughter. "Who said you get to finish?"

"So we're not fucking?"

"Yeah. I told you we weren't. You thought a few lines were going to change that? Again? You learn things, right? You're capable of it?"

Jim's mouth worked without sound for a second, and then he almost yelled, "But I wasn't finished."

"I heard. That means I win, and to the victor goes the spoils." She flashed him a grin. "In this case, the spoils are knowing you have to finish by hand."

"You're terrible."

"And for that, you don't get to look at me while you do it. Sorry."

Casting an aggravated glance in her direction, Jim jumped off his desk and scurried into the private bathroom he'd had installed. The door slammed behind him, and Rose leaned against it, listening to him pant and work.

"What do you think we should do, anyway?" she asked.

"About?"

"About the child you obviously just put in my belly? The skeleton with the goddamn fangs, moron. What do you think?"

"I'm…kinda busy."

"Jesus." Leaning against the door, she closed her eyes. Even with two lines in her system, she found coked up Jim annoying as hell. "Would it help if I talked dirty?"

"It would help if you got in here and finished me off."

"Well, let's say for the sake of argument that that isn't going to happen. I am, however, willing to call you Papi and say all sorts of disgusting things to you."

A few grunts, more panting. "Okay. Go."

So she did, exaggerating her Spanish accent and breathing heavy, giving the performance her all. Jim's grunts grew louder, and she could almost see his eyes clamped shut, his teeth bared as he struggled toward release. She faked her own orgasm as he cried out, and then she sauntered back to his desk and sat down, waiting for him.

"Big spender," she said as he left the bathroom. "Why do we do these horrible things to ourselves?"

"Enough, okay?"

"You bet, big daddy."

His smirk expressed his feelings rather well.

"So, that skeleton."

"Right," he said. "Fuck if I know what to do. Part of me wants to dig it out and display it by the entrance."

"You've got to have another idea that's not terrible."

"I don't *have* to."

"Jesus…."

Jim started cutting another pair of lines. He worked quickly and carefully, his credit card like a butcher knife as it chopped up the coke and drew it into place. "Well, I don't think we'll be doing anything with this stuff here. I guess I should probably hop online, look up protocol for this sort of thing. Gotta admit, this totally falls under the heading New Shit."

"Okay, but I don't see how the answer's going to be anything but call the police and let them take over. I don't think salvage rights apply, here."

He chuckled. "Don't try telling me dead bodies with stones jammed in their mouths don't count as salvage." Leaning forward, he placed the rolled dollar to his nostril and hit two more lines. He offered the bill to Rose, and she accepted it eagerly. As she bent and snorted her next rail, Jim fired up the computer.

She straightened, wiped at her nose. "Let me know what you find, okay?"

"Where are you going?"

"Not sleeping anytime soon. Might as well get the prep started."

Thomas spent the entire walk across the street preparing, telling himself to be ready for anything, that the old man was wild and unpredictable. By the time he reached the diner and swung open the door, he expected to find a blood bath on the other side. Instead, the scene was so close to normal it left him feeling a little sick.

He smelled bacon and heard it sizzling in the kitchen. When he looked through the order window, a pair of short order cooks worked like fine machinery. The clang of spatula against flat top griddle was almost musical. Coffee struck his nose next, a nice, thick aroma that told him he could use a cup. Sure enough, a man in work overalls sat at the counter, a mug in his hand, plate of eggs and ham in front of him like a king's feast. Another pair of diners filled one of the closest booths, a couple that ate without saying much but gave each other pleasant smiles at every opportunity. At first glance, it was almost a Rockwell painting.

But then there was the waitress. Thomas couldn't tell how old she was, because he couldn't see her face. As he walked across the diner to the booth where Jenkins sipped coffee and ate toast, all he saw of the waitress were her legs in stockings, her feet in white tennis shoes, and her rump hidden beneath the pink fabric over her uniform. She was turned away from him, her rear sticking up in the air, and the slurping sounds filled in the rest of the story before he reached the table and saw the saucer of milk.

He stood at the head of the table and watched her for a moment. She was pretty, maybe early-twenties—easily too young to be stuck in a roadside bacon-and-egg destination. Her blonde hair was pulled back in a short ponytail. If she noticed him, she gave no sign. She just kept lapping at the saucer of milk, her face happy. Every now and then, she'd rock her rump back and forth, her uniform pulling tighter.

Thomas sat down, and Jenkins looked at him.

"Did you want to say something?"

"I don't know what I could possibly say," Thomas answered.

The old man gave him the tiniest of shrugs and then took a bite of his toast. He chewed as though he knew the world would wait for him. After he swallowed, washed down the bite with a little coffee, he said, "I make you uncomfortable."

"You do." He saw no reason to lie.

"You think I shouldn't do some of the things I do?"

Thomas tried to think of the right answer. In this case, maybe a lie was the right thing. Maybe there was something in the middle, not quite the truth but not a brazen falsehood. He hoped it wouldn't anger Jenkins. Twice, he'd seen the old man lose his cool, and he still shivered when he thought about it.

"You've got seniority. It's not my place to say anything."

A dry chuckle. Jenkins watched him from over the rim of his coffee cup. Thomas saw a twinkle that was almost cruel in his eyes.

"You're still pretty new," he said. "You give it time and see. This work, it changes you. The things you thought made you happy—even the things you thought kept you from being bored—they become useless. Compared to what's out there, it's nothing."

He rubbed his fingers together and let the dust scatter again. Then, he motioned to the waitress. A quick gesture, and she reached back with one hand to hike up the bottom of her uniform. Thomas didn't want to look, but he glanced before he could stop himself. He saw white panties dotted with yellow flowers. If the woman knew what she'd done, she gave no notice, just kept working at the saucer.

"Sooner or later, something like that is going to be as necessary as your morning OJ."

"I don't think so."

"Then you're not cut out for this."

Thomas felt the frown coming, and fought back before it reached his face. Instead, he kept his expression blank, calm. He watched the old man work at his toast and coffee as though he wasn't even there, as though he had said his piece and then forgotten the rest of the world. Patiently, he waited until Jenkins finished his breakfast.

"So, where do you want to start?" he asked while Jenkins patted his lips dry with a napkin.

The old man leaned to the side and glanced at the waitress. An almost disappointed sigh eased out of him.

"At the beginning, I suppose. Let's go."

*　*　*

"So seriously, what was that?"

"Huh?" Ben snaps back into reality as the water reaches the brim of his cup. He pulls it away from the cooler and turns to face Melissa, who has a smile on her face that looks more amused than annoyed.

"The phone call, doof. What is it, three months now, and you've never called me in the middle of the night?"

"I'm aware."

Her smile widens. "So?"

"So, I'm sorry. Like I said, it was a bad dream."

"You did say that. Never told me what it was about, though."

Ben looks at her, takes in her dark, straight hair and the pale freckles on her face. She looks beautiful, and he wishes he could still tell her that. A part of him almost screams that he should tell her, but he slaps a muzzle on it. Instead, he tries to create a dream from nothing, something that would be horrible enough to warrant the call.

"It was…there was a fire, and I could hear you and the pets…."

Her face wrinkles. "That sucks."

"Like I said, it was vivid."

"But when you woke up, you had to know it was just a dream."

"Well, yeah." His throat hitches, and he feels the words trying to get out. *I was scared. I wanted to hear your voice. Every damn night, I want to hear your voice again.* He swallows them like bitter pills, and then he shrugs in a way he hopes looks playful. "I was mostly asleep. Guess my brain hadn't completely kicked in yet."

"Try waiting a few minutes next time."

"Yeah, I'll do that."

Melissa's smile widens, and for a moment he can only stare. She looks so beautiful, standing there in a hooded sweatshirt and T-shirt. Before he can stop the memory, he's back in his old kitchen, talking to her as things fall apart. They're discussing their issues and looking for some answer. Years of hidden bitterness and insecurity rush to the surface for both of them, and before he fully understands what's happening, he's saying they should split, that he should move out so they can concentrate on their friendship. He's crying, and so is she, and when they hug it's with the desperation of a drowning person clinging to anything that will keep them afloat. Later that night, he takes some blankets into the guest room—the room he'll live in for the next month—and he cries himself to sleep, telling himself he's a failure until he runs out of breath.

He returns to the break room as Melissa finishes filling her cup. When he sees that smile, he wonders how he ever could have left, and he has to remind himself their problems were more than just minor, that they'd tried to work through them and failed.

"So, yeah," he says. "I'm sorry I woke you up. Won't happen again."

"I hope not. Next time, just give it a few minutes. Grab some water or something and chill out."

"I'll give that a try."

"You better. Do it again, and you're in for a kick in the junk."

"Say no more!"

They stand there for a second, smiling at each other like fools. It feels good, and Ben is thankful they can still have these moments, that after everything else, they've stayed friends.

"I need to go mail a few things," Melissa says. She pulls a pair of envelopes from her back pocket and waves them. "Talk at you in a bit."

"Sure thing."

She leaves the break room, and he stands there for a second. Everything's quiet, and his thoughts almost rattle through his brain. At least she's safe. And she's smiling. The smile almost makes him forget about the paper sack, but then he remembers the teeth, and his good mood goes straight to hell.

Her nerves jumped, and Rose thought she could almost feel her synapses firing with every movement, every touch, every sensation she experienced. Her face remained numb, and her mouth remained dry. Smiling, she scraped her tongue against her teeth. She thought about heading to Jim's office again, grabbing a few more kisses. Just thinking about it sent sparks through her body. Or maybe that was still the coke.

Deciding it didn't matter, she went back to work on the prep. With almost stupefying speed and precision, she made short work of the vegetables that needed chopping, her knife falling into a practiced rhythm. In a few hours, Diane and Carlos would show up and wonder what they should do now that she'd handled their responsibilities, but she'd come up with something else for them. Kitchen work almost never stopped being busy, even if business had fallen from amazing to less-than-great.

More than once, her thoughts drifted to the skeleton and the stone shoved in its mouth like a gag, the fangs that held it in place. Nothing about it made sense. A part of her wanted to believe it was some kind of joke. All the other options were too easy to dismiss as superstition. Or maybe it was some psycho who'd filed his teeth down and gotten his just desserts. Maybe that was it.

She froze, the idea stuck in her brain like a thorn. The knife fell from her hand and clattered to the cutting board, and she wiped her hands on her work apron before turning and storming out of the kitchen.

Jim's office sat at the end of a short hall, branching off both the kitchen and the main floor. A bulletin board on the wall always featured the current schedule, any important news, and usually at least one photo of a drunken employee flipping off the camera. Rose blew past the board, her excitement about to erupt. Why hadn't she thought of this back when Jim first fired up the computer?

"Hey, Papi!" she said as she entered his office. "Hop on Google and see if anybody in the area ever filed down their—"

Jim was frantic. He paced back and forth, and he ran his fingers through the tight curls of his hair again and again. At first, she thought maybe he'd had one line too many, but she dismissed the idea almost immediately. Over the years, she'd seen her boss at every level from bone sober to ripped to the tits, and this was still a level beyond.

"Jim?"

He stopped pacing and turned to look at her. His face had gone white, and his mouth hung open. Wide eyes blazed with fear, and Rose found her own heart double-timing as she looked at the man's expression.

"Did you find something?" she asked.

"Huh?"

"About the skeleton, Jim. Did you find anything out?"

"Oh, yeah. Yeah. I...."

"Jim, what? What is it?"

When he shrugged, it was almost a desperate gesture, a little kid who doesn't know what else to do.

"We have to get rid of it."

"You should try honey," Jenkins said.

"What?"

"You keep blowing your nose. Allergies, right?"

Thomas stuffed his handkerchief back into his pocket. "Yeah."

"Find locally made honey. It'll boost your immunities to the pollen in the area."

He stared at the old man for a second. Was his superior really trying to be helpful? "Thanks."

"Little things. They get you through the day. You're going to be here for a while, so you might as well do everything you can."

Thomas nodded, trying to balance the man who'd just had a young woman licking milk from a saucer for his own amusement with the one who was now offering a potential allergy remedy. Maybe Jenkins was right. Years on the job might change a person. Back when he started, the old man might have been kind and caring.

No. That couldn't possibly be true.

"Are you sure we shouldn't go check those names first?" Thomas asked.

"We are. I don't intend to leave that thing in the bathroom all day, though. Housekeeping."

"Right. I just thought it would be better to move after dark."

"Too much time. Years ago, I left something similar in a hotel room. Maid came to turn down the bed, and I had even more loose ends to tie up. Let's get this one in the trunk. It'll be fine there."

"Sure it'll fit?"

"We've got a Lincoln. It'll fit just fine."

Thomas unlocked the door and stepped inside. Another groan, this one a little more urgent, greeted him.

"Sounds a little feisty," the old man said.

"Wouldn't surprise me."

"That's fine." Jenkins reached into his coat and withdrew a pistol. A pearl handle glinted in the dim light, and Thomas thought the gun looked like the heaviest weapon he'd ever seen. It dwarfed the old man's dry and wrinkled hand. Jenkins reached out and opened the bathroom door. The thing started struggling, thumping up and down as it tried to wrestle free of its binds. As casual as you please, the old man straddled the thing and placed the barrel of his pistol to its forehead.

It stopped moving. If Jenkins was pleased, his expression didn't show it. "I gather that means you know what's pressed against your skull," he said. "Good. So you can be reasoned with. My associate and I are in charge of dealing with the likes of you. You made a fun little mess, and we've also been charged with cleaning that mess. This annoys me greatly.

"Now, we're going to take you out of this room and put you in the trunk of our car. If you behave—if you remain quiet and still while we clean the mess you've made—we may decide to let you go. It's not a promise, but it's the best I can do. On the other hand, if you present a problem, we will not let you go. That is a promise, and I am not the type to break promises. If you understand, please nod."

Jenkins lifted the barrel from the thing's forehead. Slowly, it nodded.

"Very well. Thomas, would you please come in here and lift the heavier half?"

He hears Simon yowling before he even slides his key into the deadbolt. The cat desperately wants to be obese, and Ben often wonders when the yowling for food starts, if maybe his cat cries out all day, hoping a stranger will come in and give him another bowl of food. Despite his fatigue and the gnawing worry that remains on his mind, he grins as he unlocks the door and enters the apartment.

Simon scampers, racing him to the kitchen and winning by a landslide. Grumbling, Ben tosses his backpack onto the couch and follows. He tries to remember if there's an open can of food in the fridge, but the thought vanishes when he sees the paper sack sitting on the kitchen counter. The world falls into shadow around him, and all he can see is the bag. It waits like a soldier, perfectly still and patient, only this grunt is made of crinkled brown paper.

Shivers crawling up his back, Ben approaches the bag. He reaches out slowly, as though he fears it might attack. Only when his fingertips come within inches of the bag does he realize what he's doing. He snatches his hand away. There's no need for him to touch it, not when it might have evidence the police will need.

Another yowl from Simon fills the kitchen, and Ben nods. As he checks the refrigerator and grabs the can he finds inside, he fishes the cell phone from his pocket and calls the police again. A part of him thinks this is almost funny. There's a bag containing God knows what on his kitchen counter, and he's making a call and feeding his cat at the same time like it was an average weekday. If the rest of him weren't a broken, crackling wire of fear, he might laugh. Jesus, whoever left the bag got inside his apartment!

"911, emergency."

"Yeah. I've had an intruder."

"Are they still present?"

The question freezes him as he digs a fork into the brown sludge Simon eats. What if whoever delivered the bag hasn't left? Slowly, he turns and inspects the apartment around him. He sees the closed doors of the bathroom and bedroom, the tiny closet that could also hide a person. For a second, he hates that he leaves the doors shut through the day. Otherwise, he'd know someone had closed them.

"I don't know," he answers when the operator asks again.

"Sir, I need you to exit the residence, please."

He nods, forgetting the operator can't see him. When she tells him again, he says, "I'm going," and he scoops up Simon with his free arm. The cat fidgets and tries to wriggle free, but he's not letting him spend any more time alone until the police arrive. He almost makes it to the door before Simon's cries remind him of the food he left open on the counter.

"Shit." He looks at the cat squirming in the crook of his arm, at his big eyes and the hunger he sees in them.

As quick as he can, he rushes back to the kitchen and grabs the can. Then, he leaves the apartment, the emergency operator asking questions the entire time.

"What do you mean we have to get rid of it?"

Jim stared at her like she sported a baboon on her head. "I don't get what you're not understanding. We've got to take that fucking skeleton, and we have to get rid of it somehow."

"Well, you're going to have to explain it to me, because right now it just looks like you've flipped a goddamn switch. Why on God's green earth do I need to go down there, touch a fucking skeleton—one with fangs, might I add—and move it somewhere?"

Jim heaved a sigh as though he were dealing with an especially difficult child. When Rose heard it, she rolled her shoulder again. The guy might deserve a right hook after all.

"I looked it up. I mean, I looked it up the best I can. If there's more information out there, I don't know what to look for. Thing is, there's something close to a dozen state agencies that'll be interested. They'll fucking swarm this place."

"Not the restaurant. They'll be screwing around in the lakebed. That's down there, and we're up here."

Jim shook his head. He looked frustrated, like it was somehow her fault he wasn't making sense. "Look, if the right agency swoops in and thinks that skeleton is a hazard of some kind, we're looking at a nasty word, and that word is quarantine."

The word did send a hot current of anxiety through Rose's system, but she thought most of that might have been the powder. She eyed her boss, looking for any chink in his terrified armor. There had to be some spot she could hit that would make him see reason. All she saw was fear though, and the more she thought about it, the more sense it made. What he'd found in the lake wasn't an old grave site. It was a body wrapped in chains with a goddamn rock in its piehole.

"Jim, come on. It's down there. Even if they decide it is a hazard of some kind, they'll keep it contained down there. They won't even bother us."

"You can't guarantee that."

"There's no fucking flesh left on it! It's just a skeleton. Whatever was on it, fish picked clean years ago. They're not gonna shut down the entire lake."

He pointed at her, his mouth popping into an expression that said it all. *I told you so.*

"Don't, Jim."

He clasped his hands in front of his chest. When he spoke, the paranoia had left his voice. All that remained was sadness and the sincere weight of dread.

"Rose, I'm serious. You've seen what the drought has done to this place. I'm scraping by. Another few months or another kick in the balls, and we're done. I'm not talking letting a few servers go, either. I'm saying this place will die. You might be fine after that, because you're real fucking good at what you do. This place is all I have, though. You wonder how I saw that thing at two in the morning? It's because I fucking live in this office, now."

Rose nodded, because she'd been keeping quiet about that little fact for weeks. On several occasions, she'd noticed spare clothes lying around Jeff's office. She'd even seen the sleeping bag tucked under his desk. Still, she couldn't quite believe things had become so dire.

"Let's just breathe for a second, Jim. When this shit wears off, you'll feel—"

He cut her off by slamming both fists against his desk, the sound like a cannon in the tight office. "Dammit, we can't wait that long! By the time this shit is over, it'll be daylight outside. Somebody else is gonna see that fucking thing, and then it's out of our hands."

"It'll be okay!"

"You can't promise that! Goddammit, I wish you could. I really wish to hell and back that I could say everything is going to be fine. That's just not the case, though. The truth is, I don't know, and I can't take the risk of things coming down on the wrong side. Rose, I need this place. Please."

He dropped to his knees. Tears shined in his eyes. "I need your help, Rose. Please tell me you'll help me get rid of it."

Rose looked at her boss. The way he waited, his hands clasped and pleading, his expression desperate, she thought she'd never seen somebody look so honest and afraid. Before she realized what was happening, her resolve crumbled and she nodded.

"Okay. I'll help."

Thomas concentrated on breathing. In and out, in and out. It was the only thing keeping him from passing out or getting sick. He wanted to close his eyes, but he feared Jenkins would see him, and then there would be hell to pay. So, he kept watching. Even though it made him want to run screaming out of the room, he kept watching.

"What did you see?" the old man asked. "I would really like to know."

Loretta Davis had no idea her answer didn't matter. She didn't know the questions were just another way for the old man to amuse himself. Watching her thrash on the couch, he couldn't guarantee she even heard the question. She kept shrieking, swatting at her skin. A part of him wondered what Jenkins had made her see. Ants? Beetles? Snakes? He didn't know, and he had no intention of asking. With so little time on the job, his questions would probably be answered with a demonstration, and he didn't want to wind up like Mrs. Davis.

The old man leaned forward, stroking his bony chin as if deep in thought. "You see, Loretta—do you mind it I call you Loretta?"

No answer. Of course not.

"You see, Loretta, I know what you saw. You saw something you weren't meant to see. There are...we'll call them things. There are things out there that the general public just doesn't need to know about. In fact, knowing about some of these things could cause a really big problem. Panics and such. It's all nasty business, really.

"What I really need to know is if you told anyone what you saw. Now, if you can answer that question and make me believe you, I'll make all this stop. If you don't tell me, however, it's only going to get worse. Do you want this to get worse, Loretta?"

Tears streamed down her face, black lines of mascara marking her features like terrible scars. Her mouth formed into a shape like a hole, and a keening note escaped.

"Loretta?"

"No! I did't tell anybody, I...I swear!"

The old man clapped. Thomas thought the sudden celebration was almost horrifically childlike.

"That's very good, Loretta. It pleases me to hear that."

"Puh...Please."

"Please what? Make them go away?"

"Yes?"

Thomas suppressed a shiver as the old man turned to him and winked.

"Very well."

Jenkins snapped his fingers, and Loretta Davis froze, her entire body suddenly rigid. With a sound like a noise maker, her head whipped to the side, her neck cracking several times. When her body fell limp, she was looking almost directly behind her. Silence dropped over the room like a heavy curtain.

The old man stood, smacked his hands against each other as though he were brushing away dust.

"One down. Who's next?"

This time, Ben knows damn well the detective's name is Edwards. His partner goes by Randolph, and he busies himself by inspecting the apartment while Edwards starts the second hour of questioning. Again, Ben has no clue who might have left the body parts, which turned out to be a tongue and two ears. The officers who arrived first on the scene gave a good yelp when they found those particular prizes.

"I need you to really think," Edwards says. "Is there anybody you know who could do this? Who would want to do something like this?"

"No."

"Don't answer right away. Think about it a minute."

The suggestion hits him right on the annoyance button. He doesn't need a minute to think about it, because no one he knows—friend or acquaintance— is a total psychopath. Sixty seconds won't make a difference. He won't suddenly remember his friend Derrick is a medical examiner with access to body parts and an axe to grind or anything else so convenient. All he'll think about for that minute is how wonderfully normal his friends are, and then he'll probably think about how he met most of them through Melissa.

"There's no one," he says after what he hopes is an appropriate amount of time. "No one suspicious. No one with a grudge. I really have no clue."

Edwards nods, his eyes both grim and frustrated. "All right. We'll see what we can pull in the way of prints and such. Hopefully, we'll find out who's doing this. In the meantime, I'm going to have a car on you at all times."

"What?"

"Yeah. This is twice now, and even if they are just a sick prank, we can't ignore the nature of it. Believe me, it's for your safety."

Ben listens, and the detective's words make sense. The sacks have worried him, and he feels a healthy amount of fear roiling in his chest. Still, he thinks of the problems it will cause, the least of which being the fact that he's almost out of weed. Surely, the police wouldn't sit idly by as he scores. It's a terrible inconvenience, because if anything's ever made him want to smoke, it's the horrific shit that's happening to him right now.

In the next moment, he imagines a squad car sitting outside the office and the questions it will inspire. Sooner or later, it will all circle back to him, and everyone will know something weird's happening, that his life's taken a turn past pathetic and grown scary.

But then he thinks of coming home to find another brown paper sack full of human pieces. Or what if he finds one on the bedroom floor when he wakes up? Finding the most recent bag inside his apartment has made everything too close, too ripe with potential for…what? Horror? Violence? There are too many unanswered questions, and he doesn't know where to start.

"Okay," he tells the detective. "That would be great."

* * *

If Rose felt sure of anything, it was that she wasn't about to touch a skeleton that might just land them in a quarantine. She rummaged through the kitchen, grabbing garbage bags, the gloves only the newest of newbies wore, and one of the industrial rolls of plastic wrap they used for covering the prep racks. After she'd laid everything out on one of the tables, she gave it a long look, searching her mind for anything else they might need. The nerves along her spine fired like warning shots. She tried to exhale her fear, but it didn't help. How had everything turned so bizarre so fast?

Before she could stop herself, she rushed across the kitchen and ripped open the drawer where they kept the spare utensils and implements. With a shaking hand, she rummaged through the spatulas and whisks until she found one of the cheaper, rubber-handled kitchen knives. The blade wasn't terribly sharp, but it would do damage if she needed it.

"Why would I need it?" she whispered.

"Hey!" Jim slapped a hand down on one of the steel counters. "We're not exactly flush with time."

"Right. Grab what you can from that pile, and let's go."

Without a word, Jim scooped up the plastic wrap and garbage bags. He left the gloves behind, so Rose grabbed them as she moved past.

"What's with the knife?"

"It's only about a thousand percent better for cutting the wrap."

"Right, but if we wrap the entire thing, will it sink? What about air?"

She waved the knife a little. "It pokes holes, too."

"Okay, yeah."

She let her boss lead, sticking close as they left the restaurant and made their way to the docks. Jim insisted on no lights, and she had to admit it was a good idea. Getting caught moving a skeleton sat at the bottom of her favorite things list.

"How much time do we have left?" she asked.

"Hour and a half. Maybe a little less."

"Shit. And we have to row this thing out?"

"Yeah. Sucks, don't it?"

Rose tried to picture the two of them in a damn canoe, paddling out into the middle of Lake Travis while sharing space with a dead body. She hated thinking about the cramped quarters, because she didn't care that there wasn't so much as a scrap of tissue left on those bones. She didn't care that they planned to wrap it in plastic so they wouldn't have to make any real contact with it. At the heart of it all, they'd be spending time with a corpse, and that was something she could barely comprehend, let alone stomach.

Climbing the ladder down to the lakebed was a challenge. The darkness felt thicker as dawn approached, and her jangling nerves made the process of feeling for the next rung with her toes something close to a thrill ride. When she finally dropped to the ground, her breath came in ragged bursts.

"You okay?" Jim asked.

"Fine. Let's just do this."

"Right. Once we grab things, we won't worry about the ladder. We'll take the long way around and just climb the bank. Probably be easier."

"Whatever. Let's go."

Jim's footsteps trailed away. She followed, and she reached for the knife's handle. Her fingers tightened, and she felt a little better. At least she had a weapon.

"Please tell me it's still there," she said.

"It is."

Jim stood over the bound skeleton, and Rose found herself staring at the skull. She wondered if it had belonged to a man or woman, if they'd been alive when the stone was shoved past their teeth. It must have felt terrible. The thought of experiencing that kind of horror made her eyes water. As she dried them with the heel of her hand, she thought about the fangs. Could they be real? If they were, could the skeleton really be human?

"Jesus."

"Nope," Jim answered. He sat the box of plastic wrap beside the skeleton's legs. "Afraid he ain't here to help. Now, let's get this over with."

By the time they reached the last house, Thomas thought every breath tasted like cold dirt. He could only look straight ahead. For several moments, he examined the street and the curb, hoping Jenkins would remain silent, maybe even show some kind of mercy.

The truth stared him in the face: he wasn't cut out for the job. In the hidden corners of his mind, he'd always known, but he'd done a good job of lying to himself. For months now, he'd told himself falsehood after falsehood, each fiction a piece of the façade that showed the old man and everybody else he was meant to be a fixer. He wasn't sure when the cracks had started to show, but he knew the moment the entire work had shattered.

Thomas closed his eyes. He knew his fingers were iron around the steering wheel, that he was all but shaking in the Lincoln's seat, but he couldn't control it. Theresa Davis had been the third name on the list, and her voice still reverberated in his memory.

She'd said, "Please."

"Please."

The first time, he'd barely been able to understand her. She blubbered, and the wet sound of her pain and terror transformed the word into something more sensation than speech. One hand reached for them, palm up, the flesh raw and pulpy, portions of it still lodged in her teeth or hanging in slick clumps around her lips. She said the magic word again, this time her voice almost a shriek, and then she pressed the hand to her mouth and took another bite.

"How long do you think it will take?" Jenkins had asked. There was no smile on his face, no horrible glint in his eye, and that somehow made it all worse. He wasn't enjoying himself; he was curious.

Mrs. Davis ate most of her right arm before the trauma killed her. On the back of his eyelids, Thomas watched her body flop and buck against the floor like a sick imitation of grease in a skillet.

"I want you to handle this one."

He opened his eyes at the sound of the old man's voice. Thankfully, he hadn't started or gasped in any way. It took him a second to make sense of the words, but once he understood them his body went cold with dread.

"What?"

"You heard. You know."

"I..." Again he looked to the street, hoping something out there might distract him. There was nothing, though. A quiet street on a quiet day. Damn.

"I don't believe I'm ready." His voice quivered, and he hated it.

"That's quite unfortunate. I don't want you thinking you have a choice in the matter."

Thomas blinked. He turned to face Jenkins, found him looking out the window at the house that held Doris Hubbert, the last name he'd given the old man.

"I'm sorry?"

"You've been coasting. People have noticed. The word has come down that you need to step up to the plate. You're not performing as you should, and you have no choice but to improve. Like it or not, you signed a contract, and that means you have obligations."

Thomas remembered signing, remembered the dry scratch of the pen on paper. Earlier, the old man's pencil had made the same noise. He recalled the heavy, suffocating despair that had filled him at the time, and how hopeless and gray and wounded the world had seemed, bloody slashes across his mind and his heart. He wondered if Jenkins had felt the same as he signed his contract.

"I don't—"

A dry, firm hand appeared on his wrist. This time, he did start, and the hand clamped down like a vice.

Thomas looked into the old man's eyes. Anger brewed there like stormclouds.

"This is our job," Jenkins said. "This is what we *do*."

Slowly, Thomas nodded. He knew in that moment that the world was still hopeless, that his wounds hadn't healed and may never. But that didn't change anything. The old man was right.

"I'll do it," he said.

"Has anything weird happened, lately?"

Standing in the break room, Melissa gives him a look like he's just asked if she'd considered adopting a man-eating donkey for a pet. Her eyes narrow, and then a sarcastic grin creeps across her face. "Like hanging out with my ex? Yeah, I guess that one happens a lot."

"Not quite what I was going for, but good to know."

"What's going on?"

He stands there for a moment, dipping a teabag into a mug of hot water and wondering how much he should reveal. Scaring her is the last thing he wants, but if somebody has it in for him, they might decide to make life hell for everybody else in his life. The thought of Melissa experiencing what he's gone through feels like a barbed spike in his chest.

So he tells her everything. He starts with the knock on the door and takes her through all of it, finishing with the police car that waits in the parking lot, the officers inside doing their best to keep an eye on him. Her expressions start with amusement and anticipation before taking a sharp turn into shock and horror and finally settling on genuine concern with a healthy amount of fear. When he finishes, he stands there and waits for her to say something. The silence remains for a long time, and he wonders if she'll say anything or just storm away.

"Holy shit," she finally says

They're the same words that have buzzed around his cranium for days. Few things sum up the bizarre turn his life has taken as well as those words. He nods, giving Melissa a look that says he knows exactly what she means.

She sets down her drink and throws her arms around him before he can think to reach. In the circle of her arms, it feels like home, and he wants to return her embrace, but there's still a mug of hot tea in his hand. "Okay," he says. "All right, don't make me spill this."

"Why didn't you tell me sooner?" She steps back, and he sets down his mug before she can change her mind.

"I don't know. I called because I was concerned, but then I just...I guess I didn't want to bother you."

"Bother me?"

"It's not the best way to word it."

"No, it isn't. Bother me? What kind of a bitch do you think I am?"

"Did I say that at some point?" he asks.

"You know what I mean."

"And I'd hoped you would know what I mean."

She grins. "Well, you used the wrong words."

The laughter bubbles out of him before he knows its coming. It feels good, the surge in his chest and belly. How long has it been since he really laughed? Soon, he stands with his hands on his knees, fighting for air as the laughter tumbles free.

He looks up and sees Melissa join him. The smile on her face is enormous and natural, and he thinks it's the most beautiful she's ever looked. He wants to watch her smile all day, but then her expression changes, becoming harder. The change is so fast, it feels as though her happy expression has been torn away.

"You didn't just leave Simon in the apartment, did you?"

Her words hit him like a slap from a cold hand. For a second, all he can do is stare at her with what he's sure is an idiot's expression. Why hadn't he thought to take Simon somewhere else? Jesus, the cat had been in the apartment when somebody left a bag full of ears on the kitchen counter! He wonders if Simon hid or if the intruder simply didn't care. In the next second, his mind shows him pictures of his cat dead, maybe stuffed inside the refrigerator or strewn across the living room as some kind of horrible message.

"Can I take him to…your place?" Referring to the house as anything other than home still feels alien.

"Of course," Melissa says. "Do it fast, though. Shit!"

He nods and rushes past her.

Preparing the body for dumping took longer than Rose expected. Jim tried to wrap the entire thing in one go, but the bones didn't want to stay together. For ten minutes, she watched as her boss fumbled and fussed and cursed before he finally grew too frustrated and started stomping on it. Bones splintered. The legs fell apart, followed by the arms. The thing's ribcage collapsed into a pile of thin bones and vertebrae. Rose watched it all, shivering. Jim probably wanted help, but breaking apart dead bodies didn't fall within her job description.

After several minutes, Jim stopped his demolition. He stood over the shattered skeleton with his hands on his sides, sucking wind. When he looked at her, an embarrassed smile appeared below his eyes.

"Some fun, huh?"

"Looked like a blast."

A groan crawled out of him, and then he rubbed his face with both hands, trying to clear away the sweat that beaded there. "Good thing you thought to bring those garbage bags. Gonna make this a lot easier."

"Yeah, it will. Kinda embarrassed we didn't think about disassembling that damn thing, though."

He shrugged. "We can't all be geniuses. Or is it geni?"

"Does that even sound real to you?"

"Excellent point. Okay, let's glove up and do this shit."

The gloves felt like faulty armor over her hands. Looking at the pile of bones and the chain, Rose thought she wanted a whole lot more than a single layer of latex protecting her. As she pulled the gloves over her hands, she wondered how doctors and surgeons could stand to trust such a thin layer of protection. Maybe it had something to do with them not being ripped on coke. Clean living probably shut down paranoia pretty well.

Jim shook out one of the garbage bags and handed it to her. She took it and stared at the skeleton, trying to decide where to start while Jim opened a second bag. After a moment of thoughts that left her shivering, she crouched and picked up one of the thing's feet. Through the latex, the bones felt brittle and impossibly light. A part of her mind wondered if maybe it was a prank, if maybe somebody had dropped a convincing replica in the lake as a sick joke. Then, she thought maybe Jim had done it just a few hours ago, thinking was really fucking hilarious. She looked at her boss with a glare in her eyes, but he looked disgusted as he plucked bones from the ground and dropped them into his bag.

They worked in silence until they were done. Every time she thought they were finished, she spotted another bone. When she went close to a minute without finding one, she risked using her cigarette lighter to provide a tiny pocket of illumination. It revealed more bones, pieces and splinters that they retrieved like criminals scooping butts from highway shoulders.

"I think that's everything," Jim said in a weary voice. He picked up the chain and let it rattle its way into his garbage bag.

"You're right."

"Not a lot of dark left. Think there's a spot in the walk-in we can stash this until tonight?"

"No."

"Not even—"

"Health department, porters, prep cooks, servers running in to get more creamer. Too many risks, so no."

Jim tied his bag shut and set it on the ground. He stretched, and Rose heard his back pop in a few places. "Okay. Let's shag ass, then."

When Doris Hubbert opened her door, Thomas knew at once that she remembered the thing in the bag.

It was written al over the expression that was both terrified and exhausted. He wondered how poorly she'd been sleeping, and then he wondered why she hadn't simply skipped town. The answer appeared in his mind a second later. Sometimes frightened people just turtle up. Doris hadn't fled for the same reason the other three hadn't: they were too damn scared.

"Miss Hubbert?"

"Yes?"

"Hello. My name is Gregory Thomas, and this is my partner. We're with The Department of Wildlife and Natural Resources."

She watched him expectantly, half her body hidden behind the door.

"We were hoping we might be able to come in and speak with you for a minute."

"What about?"

"Well ma'am, we've had some coyotes spotted in the area—coming down out of the hill country, we imagine—and we were hoping to talk to you a bit about what to do, should one wander onto your property."

"Oh. Well, wouldn't I just call animal control?"

"I'm afraid not. See...these particular animals are protected by various Texas agencies, and we've found animal control tends to operate on more of a lone wolf philosophy. The average animal control worker is a thug. They're more likely to beat or kill the animal than to contain it and return it to the wild."

"I didn't know that," she said. Sadness appeared in her eyes. Maybe a little outrage, too.

"Most citizens don't. It's one of those truths that likes to stay...tucked away."

"Oh."

Thomas felt the old man's gaze on his back, chilling him like a layer of frost. "May we?" he asked, gesturing toward the door. Doris eyed them for a second, and then she stepped back and opened the door the rest of the way.

"Of course. Come in."

Thomas breathed deep as he walked through the door. He needed to steel himself. As he nodded a thank you at Doris Hubbert, he wondered how he'd wound up in this awful line of work in the first place. The answer was a simple one, and he knew it. Some people screw up so badly they have nowhere else to go. He'd done exactly that, and now he got to spend the rest of his life doing things like this, moving through Texas with Jenkins and cleaning up messes that needed cleaning.

Doris led them into the living room and asked if they wanted tea or coffee. He said he was fine, but Jenkins wanted coffee, black. As she puttered out of the room, her eyes active and searching, he examined the place. It was quaint. Tasteful wallpaper covered the walls, and the couch was clean, the carpets recently vacuumed. An upright piano stood against one wall, and a black and white photo hung above it showed a respectable-looking couple. Her parents, he guessed. Or maybe her husband's.

Heat flared through him as he remembered Doris Hubbert was married. He wondered if she'd told her husband what she'd seen, if he'd believed her or told her she was being hysterical. With his next thought, he wondered how her husband would react when he came home. He doubted it would be a nice scene.

Doris returned, a ceramic mug in her hand. She crossed the room and handed it to Jenkins, who muttered his thanks as he accepted the cup. Thomas thought about the last time he'd seen the man drink coffee, about the waitress hiking her skirt up to expose her panties, and he felt ill. Would he really end up like the old man? He hated the idea.

Doris sat in a recliner on the other side of the room. She still looked worried, but she appeared to have calmed some. "So what should I do if I see one of these coyotes?"

Thomas started to speak, but Jenkins cleared his throat. It was a harsh sound, and he knew it was supposed to be a reminder of what they'd come to do. A deep breath eased out of him, and the knot that was his guts tightened a little bit. Fine, he could do this, even if he hated it.

"Well, Mrs. Hubbert, I'm afraid we need you to do something for us."

Her face darkened with worry. "I'm sorry? What do you mean?"

Thomas swallowed, and it felt like a lump of ice travelling down his throat.

"I'm afraid we need you to kill yourself."

Ben works only a few miles from the apartment, but the drive feels like an eternity. He runs through lights and cuts off other cars. A chorus of angry horns chases him down the street, but he doesn't care. A part of his mind tells him it's ridiculous to do this for a cat, but

113

the rest of him sees Simon's face, wide eyes full of love and need. He hears the cat's purr, his hungry yowls that wake him up just after three o'clock every morning, and he thinks to himself that the cat is the only family he has left. The gray and black feline is important. He represents that last vestige of normalcy, and Ben refuses to let anything bad happen to him.

He turns his car into the apartment complex with a screech, one of the rear wheels hopping the curb and crashing back down. As he swerves through the parking lot, racing for his building, he mutters a prayer. *Please let Simon be okay.* If something happens to the cat, he doubts he can cope.

Finally, he reaches his building and cuts his car into the first parking space he sees. Yanking his keys from the ignition, he doesn't bother locking the car as he slams the door shut behind him. His steps thunder up the stairs. He races past the second floor to the third, and the climb feels like forever. The final charge down the hallway to his apartment takes just as long, and he pants as he stands in front of his door and looks for the key that will unlock it. Twice, his numb fingers drop the key ring, and he mutters a curse as he snatches them from the ground. When he finally finds the right key, he slams it into the lock.

And then he hears a sneeze on the other side of the door. Suddenly, everything feels cold and distant, and he knows whoever has been leaving the paper sacks is in his apartment right now. Fear makes him shake, but the emotion slowly twists into rage. It's gone too far. He doesn't like being afraid, and now he can do something about it. Casting a glance over his shoulder, he wonders if the team meant to keep an eye on him has followed him home, and he wonders if they'll enter his apartment before whatever will happen takes place. As these thoughts play out, he wraps his fist around his keyring, letting the keys jut from between his fingers. Fuck it.

He throws open the front door.

"Shit." The voice sounds annoyed, even tired. It comes from an old man in a suit. He stands in the center of the living room, stuffing a handkerchief into his pocket. A paper sack fills his other hand. "Cedar, right? Gets me right in the sinuses. Sorry. You weren't supposed to see this."

Ben steps into the apartment. "Where's my cat?"

"Asleep in the corner. I didn't touch him. I think he might have a skin condition; he's licking and chewing on his tail too much. Cute cat, though. Simon, right?"

"Uh...yeah." Against his better judgment, Ben closes the door behind him and throws the deadbolt. Something about the old man's voice puts him at a strange sort of ease. Maybe it's how fatigued the man sounds, or maybe it's the weary expression that fills his face. Even though he knows he should fear this man who's been leaving him grisly presents, he just can't bring himself to do it.

The old man sits on the couch, sighing as though the simple act of standing was too much. He rubs his hands over his legs. His suit looks old. "I suppose you have questions," he says.

"Bet your ass."

"All right. Go ahead."

"Sure thing." He crosses the living room floor until he's standing over the man, only the coffee table separating them. The key ring bites into his tight fist. "First off, who the fuck are you?"

The old man nods as though he's always expected this question. "My name is Gregory Thomas. At this point, I usually tell people I work for some state agency. That's when I want to get into their home, though. You already caught me here, so I might as well tell you the truth."

"Just like that?"

A shrug. He looks even more exhausted than when Ben first entered.

"So what's the truth?" Ben asks.

"The truth is I fix things when they go wrong."

"Really? Is that what you do?"

"Sincerely. Somebody has to do it."

"So what went wrong that can only be fixed with paper bags full of body parts?"

Gregory Thomas looks at him. One corner of his mouth ticks upward. "I think you know."

Rose made Jim row, because she was busy hugging herself to keep from shivering in the chilly air that descended over Lake Travis. The gentle sounds of the oar slicing through water was almost relaxing, but the two garbage bags taking up space in the bottom of the canoe counteracted that particular lullaby.

"How much farther, do you think?" she asked.

The rowing sound stopped as Jim turned around to gauge their distance from the bank. "Let's go another fifty yards. After that, I think it would take another four years of drought for this crap to get found."

"I hope so."

"At a certain point, I think hope is all we have left. Jesus, I wish I had some more coke." He shoved the oar into the water again.

"Because that's what you need right now."

"I didn't hear you complaining earlier."

"That was well before I got slapped with body disposal duty," Rose said.

"Everybody's a goddamn critic. I'll make it up to you, okay?"

"You better."

"Just tell me how."

She thought about it a second. "The Killers are playing Frank Erwin next month. I want tickets and the night off."

"The fucking Killers?"

"Yeah."

"Fine. Jesus Christ." He flattened out his oar, and the canoe sliced to the right before coming to a stop. Looking around, he lifted the wood from the water and laid it across the boat. "I think this'll do it."

"At last. So do we just toss these?" She looked at the bag by her feet and tried to forget what was inside. A few hours ago, she'd just been a chef with a fondness for various drugs. Now, she was dumping a body that was God knows how old and just might have belonged to some kind of monster. She hoped she could course correct after such a strange left turn.

"Guess so. Tear some holes so it sinks."

"Sure thing." She took hold of the bag closest to her and ripped a pair of holes in it with the kitchen knife. The air inside whispered out, and she thought it smelled old, stale. Maybe it was her imagination, but she couldn't be sure. There was too much weirdness in the moment to be certain.

She heaved her bag over the side. There was a splash, followed by another as Jim did the same with his. By the dying moonlight, she watched the bag float on the water's rippling surface for a moment. Then, they began to sink. A bubbling sound drifted upward as the black plastic disappeared beneath the water. Soon, the lake was still again, and they were alone in the quiet.

"That's that, I guess," she said. She turned to Jim, and she saw a strange look on his face. "What is it?"

"Can I trust you?" he asked.

"What?"

"No one can ever know what we just did. You know that, right? I need to know I can trust you to keep it a secret."

"Jim, you know I can."

"Do I?"

His hands wrapped around the oar's wooden handle, and Rose thought she saw his knuckles whiten with the effort. She thought about the knife that now rested in her lap. How fast could she grab it?

"Jim, come on. How long have I worked with you? I could have left at any point this year, once business started going downhill. Did I do that? Nope. I believed in you. So, believe in me. You're not the only one who would get in trouble if this got out. Think about it."

Rose watched as he did just that. For a moment that

felt like hours, he watched her, and she could almost see him inch toward his decision. She shifted her hand closer to the knife's handle, but then Jim let go of the oar and held up his hands. He shook his head, his expression apologetic and embarrassed.

"You're right. Sorry. I just...fucked up night, y'know?"

She sighed and then smiled. "Yeah. I know."

"You want to head back?"

"More than ever."

"All right, then." He scooped up the oar and stabbed it into the water. Grunting with the effort, he turned around the canoe and got them moving toward the shore again.

They wound through the hills around Lake Travis until they found a secluded spot. Thomas piloted the bulky Lincoln down a road that was little more than two gravel ruts gouged in the ground. He drove in silence, his face grim. In his mind, he saw Doris Hubbert cry as she took the kitchen knife in her hand and dug it deep into first one forearm and then the other, opening herself up so she could bleed to death on the kitchen floor. He hadn't looked at Jenkins then, and he hadn't looked at him since. For all he cared, the old man could die or disappear or burst into flames and burn into nothing but ashes. Thinking about the perverse bastard left him feeling sick.

Finally, the Lincoln exited the woods, and Thomas saw the waters of Lake Travis lapping at the shore. The sun had set, but complete dark hadn't arrived. It didn't matter much. They had one last piece of business to attend to, and then they'd go their separate ways until the next mess needed fixing.

Thomas killed the lights and then the engine. For a long time, he sat perfectly still, hands on the wheel, looking out at the black water. He searched deep in his soul and wondered if he could keep doing this or if maybe he should take the route he'd convinced Doris Hubbert to take. Maybe that would be easier. Hell, maybe it was just the right thing to do.

"I had the same thoughts when I first started," Jenkins said.

Thomas blinked. Slowly, he turned to look at the man. He was gazing out the window as he lit a cigarette.

"Can you…?"

"What?" Jenkins asked. "Can I read minds? Don't need to when it's written all over your face like that."

Thomas rubbed his face with both hands. "I just don't know if I can handle this."

"I know. Nobody does. You have to, though. Simple as that."

"What we did today—not what we did, but how we did it—it's cruel."

The old man inhaled and then blew a plume of blue smoke out his window. "It's necessary. Don't confuse the two."

"We could have snapped their necks without saying a word."

"Wouldn't look convincing, not with four in the same day."

"Guns, knives."

"Sloppy. Room for error." Abruptly, the old man shouldered open his door and climbed out before leaning his head into the car. "Come on. You need to see this."

"See what?"

"Come on."

Thomas climbed out of the Lincoln and followed Jenkins to the trunk. The soles of his shoes scraped over the rocky shore, the sound like ghosts moving through the canyon. When he reached the trunk, the old man wrenched it open. The chained bag waited inside, the thing inside beginning to move again.

With surprisingly nimble fingers, Jenkins untied the drawstring at the top of the canvas sack and opened it, pulled it down to reveal the face of the thing they'd been transporting all day.

The dying light somehow still reflected off the bone white face that looked just removed from humanity. From within deep, shadowed sockets, its eyes burned orange and red. Past its black and desiccated lips, Thomas saw the broken teeth and the fangs, the stone he'd shoved in its mouth to keep it from biting any more humans. The thing hissed past the obstruction in its mouth, and it was a sound of both hunger and hate.

"Look at it," Jenkins said. "Take a good, hard look. Our job is to make sure things like this stay hidden. The world isn't nearly ready for something like this. What we do, it isn't pretty, but it's necessary.

"We kill people because we have to, and over the years it will get shockingly easy. What we can do, we can do for a reason. The job gives us terrible powers so we can do terrible things. It makes us a little more than a regular person, though. The longer you do this job—and believe me, you're stuck with it—the harder it's going to be for you to feel like a human and not something like this. Or something like me."

Jenkins reached out. Thomas flinched and then regained his composure as the old man's dry palm pressed against his heart.

"Do what you can, Gregory Thomas. Hold onto this as long as possible. You're in this job forever, but try to remember that it's just a job. It's not what you are. We get downtime between incidents. Use it wisely. Save puppies, for all I care. Just remember that when you're on the clock, you're on the clock."

Thomas nodded. He thought he saw sadness in the old man's eyes, but he couldn't be sure. Silently, he watched as Jenkins drew the bag over the hissing beast's head and pulled the string taught once again.

"All right," the old man said. "Let's sink this thing and go home."

Ben stares at Gregory Thomas, who sits on the couch with his legs spread, wrists resting on his knees and hands hanging down. The old man looks like a big kid, a child who grew up before his time. Between them, a paper sack sits on the coffee table, a dark stain along the bottom.

"What do you mean I know what went wrong?" he asks the intruder.

"You've known for a while," Gregory Thomas says.

"Apparently not."

"You cry yourself to sleep a few times every week. You sit here and sulk. Every now and then you try to go out and prove you can function like this, but it doesn't work out, does it? And you still talk to her. Every single day, you still talk to her."

Ben feels himself sink into sad thoughts. He wants to protest, but he knows the man is right. Maybe he thought he'd be better alone, but now he has doubts. They creep into his thoughts every day, and he can't chase them off no matter how hard he tries.

"What does that have to do with the bags?"

The man's head cocks to one side and then rights itself. "Who did you call that first night? You wanted to make sure she was all right. Who did you tell everything to once you couldn't keep it bundled up anymore? Like it or not, she's a part of you, and you're a part of her. And the two of you fit together very well. It's not perfect, but it never is. No matter how much we want it to be, sometimes as good as it gets is, well…as good as it gets."

Ben feels a little dizzy. He can't quite believe everything. The bags, the man on his couch: it's all too surreal, and it's sent the entire world spinning.

"What's in that bag?" he finally asks.

"In here?" The man picks up the bag and hefts it. "A few more teeth. A finger."

"What? Where are you getting this stuff?"

He holds up a hand, telling him to take it easy. "It's not one of hers, so what does it matter? She's still waggling all ten. When the police run it, however, they won't find any matches."

Ben stares at the man. He stares and tries to make some kind of sense out of it all.

"Wait a second…why the bags at all? You could have sent a goddamn card or something!"

"I've been fixing things a long time. For the most part, it's pretty gruesome work. Sometimes you get stuck in old habits. It affects these little…side projects."

"Old habits?"

Gregory Thomas stands. Ben steps back, the reaction sudden and full of fright.

"Yes, old habits. Try not to get stuck in your own."

Thomas reaches out and places a hand on his chest. Ben feels his heart thud against it, a bass drum.

"Do what you can, Ben. Hold onto this as long as possible. You fall into bad habits, you might never break free. Take it from an old man."

He tries to think of a reply, a retort. Instead, he stands in stunned silence as the man shakes the bag a few times.

"I'll just take this with me. I don't think you need it."

Gregory Thomas reaches the door and pauses, hand on the knob. "One thing…."

"Yeah?"

"No one ever finds out about this. I mean it. You even consider telling somebody, and you'll either see me again or somebody who isn't quite as nice. It won't be a good meeting. Understand?"

"Um…sure. I understand."

"Good."

The man leaves, shutting the door behind him, and Ben continues to stand there. In his mind, he sees Melissa's face. She smiles, and the tears rush to his eyes. He wipes at them with trembling fingers, and then he fishes his phone from his pocket and gives her a call.

* * *

Rose slept late. Exhaustion had woven itself through every inch of her body. When she opened her eyes, the sun was bright and streaming through her window, something she hadn't seen in longer than she could remember. Panic rushed in, but then she remembered that Jim had told her to sleep in, that after their night and then a full shift, she deserved a day of sleep. He'd place the call to her sous chef personally.

She looked at the clock and saw it was just past ten. Screw it. She'd grab a few more hours. Not like she hadn't earned them.

Sleep had almost taken hold again when somebody knocked on her door. At first, she tried to ignore it. If it wasn't the mailman dropping off a package, it was probably Jim wanting to talk about what they'd done. She doubted she had the strength for such a discussion. Maybe in a few hours.

The knock came again, a little louder, but no more urgent. In that moment, it dawned on her that it might be the police. Panic fluttered in her chest as her eyes snapped open again. She sat up and leaped out of her bed. Looking down, she saw she was wearing a T-shirt and little else.

"Coming!" she called. As quickly as she could, she climbed into a pair of jeans. Looking out her window, she saw a few cars, but nothing that looked like a squad car or even a detective's sedan. Her heart slowed, and her breath came a little easier. Probably the mailman, maybe Jim. She wouldn't know until she checked.

She walked barefoot across the fake wood flooring of her living room. The early morning chill bit at her, but she didn't mind. It wasn't like she was still asleep.

The knock came a third time.

"Goddammit, I'm here." She twisted the deadbolt and then the thumb lock on the doorknob. If it was the mailman, the delivery had better be spectacular.

A man who looked to be well into his seventies waited on the other side of her door. He wore an old, slightly wrinkled suit. When he gave her a pleasant smile, she thought she caught a hint of sadness in his eyes.

"Hello?"

"Good morning," the man said. "My name is Gregory Thomas, and I'm with The Department of Health and Human Services. May I come in for a moment?"

DEEPER WATERS

"You smell that?"

"What are you talkin' about?"

"You can't smell it? It's the morning, the sun hitting the world and waking everything up."

"No, I don't guess I smell it."

"Figures. Something's all around you, and you can't even tell it's there."

"Maybe it's the river, Charlie."

"I know what the goddamn river smells like. This is something different. It's something powerful, vital. It's like sniffing life."

"You say so. All I can breathe is that green fuckin' water."

Charlie Crawford--"Charlie Crawdad" to his friends and "that rotten asshole" to just about everybody else-- leaned out the open floor-length window and looked at the flooded street below. The thick, oily river water was at least five feet high now, probably closer to seven or eight. He ran his fingers through his short black curls and shook his head, a smile spreading across his thin lips. When the Ohio spilled her banks, she did it fast and with gusto.

"I think she's angry," he said. He blinked a memory away before returning his attention to the man at his side.

Jimmy Mills shot a glance at the flooded street. "You mean the river?"

"I do."

"What's it got to be pissed off about?"

"Ain't an 'it,' Jimmy. The Ohio's a 'she.' Always has been. If you realized that, maybe you'd know why she's pissed."

"Because chicks are always pissed?"

"See? That's why you're single."

"You're single too, asshole."

"Because I choose to be. Folks--especially women--have a habit of getting hurt when they get too close to me."

"That so?"

"In my experience."

"You sayin' I'm gonna get hurt, Charlie?"

"Who knows? We ain't that close."

"You decided to hole up here and wait the flood out."

"You're paying me to make sure your place don't go all Atlantis on ya. Not exactly the same thing."

"Whatever." Jimmy leaned out the window and spit a long stream of crud into the water below. "So why is she pissed then?"

Charlie's smile looked like a block of ice. "Still haven't figured it out?"

"Why don't you tell me?"

"And keep you from learnin' something? No way in hell. Now come on. Let's go downstairs and have a look."

A shadow of worry crossed Jimmy's regularly handsome features. It almost matched the shadow cast by his River City Rollerderby cap. "You sure that's--"

Charlie slapped him across the back, his smile stretching. "Shit yeah, it's a good idea! We used grave ash, didn't we? You and I both know there ain't shit gonna bust through that."

"You're probably right."

"Probably? I oughta feed you your own ass, you wave probably at me. C'mon, you frightened little bastard. Let's go downstairs and have a look."

Charlie tried not to laugh at the frightened expression Jimmy wore like an especially ugly mask. If the man wanted to piss himself, he didn't need to be snickered at for it. But hell, if Jimmy was still scared even after he'd brought Charlie in to shore the place up, then getting his panties up in a bunch was the least of the man's worries.

The thought did bring a chuckle to Charlie's lips. If Jimmy had any idea...

The sound of water scraping against the storefront's brick reached his ears seconds before his foot touched down on the kitchen's linoleum floor. Jimmy's Diner--The Spot--wasn't much, but it was functional. The ovens hadn't blown up on anybody, and the grill only burned the hamburgers half the time. Didn't appear to affect Jimmy's wallet at all. The Spot did a real crackerjack business, and Charlie seriously doubted any of Jimmy's regulars would stay away if they saw the state of the cramped kitchen. As long as the food tasted good--which it did through some strange miracle--the fine folks of Sulfer, Indiana probably wouldn't give a good goddamn.

"Floor looks dry," Jimmy said, voice echoing with anxiety.

"Take her easy." He shook his head. At this rate, the guy was gonna have a heart attack before the water pulled back into the river. That wouldn't do anybody a lick of good.

"I'm just saying."

"Well, just stop. What is it, Jimmy? You don't trust me or something?"

"I trust you fine. It's the damn river I'm not too keen on."

"Pussy." He shook his head, hiding the smirk plastered across his mug, and pushed through the door into the dining room.

A shimmering green shadow filled the small room, clinging to the four booths that lined either wall and draping over the old juke box pressed against the lunch counter. What light made it through the swollen river felt thick and oppressive, like an imitation of the Ohio herself. You could swim through the dining room just the same as you could swim through the polluted water, only one was nowhere near as dangerous as the other.

Charlie eyed the door, the floor beneath it. Not a drop of water had pushed through the entry. Good to know he still had the mojo working full bore.

"Good work," Jimmy said.

"No thing." He let a healthy amount of ego creep into his voice. Why not?

"Not sure I would've trusted anybody else in town to get it done."

"Please. It's an old trick, Jimmy, and just about everybody in Sulfer knows it. Not like I invented grave ash or some shit."

"Nah, but you're part of the river."

That did drag a laugh out of him.

"What?" Jimmy asked. The word was all but lost beneath Charlie's guffaws and the creaks and groans of water against brick and glass. "Seriously, Charlie. What?"

"Part of the river? What the hell you talking about?"

A twist of annoyance appeared in Jimmy's eyes. "Don't play dumb on me, man. Everybody knows. You were conceived in the Ohio. The river's part of you, and you're part of it."

"You're half-right, Jimmy. My parents were in the Ohio when my daddy was balls-deep in my mama, and if that's when I was conceived, then there mighta been some greasy river water up in there with me. Don't make me anything other than a man who knows a few tricks, though. You've lived here all your life. You know everybody's got at least one good trick in 'em. Hell, man, you know a trick or two."

Jimmy shook his head. "Not like you, though."

Charlie's smile showed his teeth, a dull yellow brought on by years of coffee and smokes. He slapped The Spot's owner across the shoulder. "I wouldn't be too sure, my friend. I think you got some surprises in store. Yup, think you got at least one good turn in ya."

He fished a hand into his pocket, and it returned with a pack of Marlboro's. He screwed one into his lips and lit it. He let the first puff hang in his lungs before blowing it back into Jimmy's face.

"Probably shouldn't be smoking that right now."

"Probably not," he said through grinning lips. "Might piss off the other customers." He swung his arms wide, blew another plume of smoke through a shit-eating grin.

Jimmy watched, his face blank.

He shrugged and pinched the smoke out between two fingers. "How about a burger, Jimmy? I'm damn hungry after making you safe as houses."

"Sure. I'll get on it. Can't do fries, though. Only used enough magic to keep the grill going."

"I'm sure I'll just weather through and somehow find the strength to survive."

"Fine."

"Tell me how much you love me, Charlie."

"More than a little. Almost as much as a fifty-dollar lapdance."

He smiled as Tammie punched his arm and called him a rotten prick. The girl had a way with words, and it always pulled a grin across his lips.

"You always gonna treat me so bad?" she asked through a pout.

He touched his fingers to her cheek. "I'll make you a deal. If I ever start treating you bad, you just let me know and I'll take it out of my own hide."

Her smile was a candle along the darkness of the riverbank.

Charlie jerked awake, hating himself more than a little.

* * *

A sour grimace hung over Charlie's face as he listened to the sizzling of ground beef on hot metal. Getting the grill to fire up when the town was under seven feet of water was about as close as Jimmy got to having a talent. Time would tell if the man held any further value. Charlie figured if anybody could wring it out of the man, it was him.

He turned up his nose and sniffed a few times. He caught the faintest whiff of seasoned meat, but he smelled something else underneath--something raw and sick. Bad shit in the air. Nothing new, really. Sulfer wasn't exactly Disney World. Nasty things happened all the damn time in the four street by four street Indiana burg. Some would say it was their stock in trade. Some folks even believed it, too, but there was a word for those folks: fucking stupid. Anybody who bought a dollar of their own bullshit deserved to drown in a puddle of it, and Charlie Crawdad had seen just such an occurrence on at least four separate occasions.

Just one benefit to being a magician.

He turned to look over his shoulder. The water flowed slowly past the glass storefront. He watched clumps of plants and muck tumble along on the lazy, pulsing current. Probably wouldn't be too long until some of the other river inhabitants made themselves known. Hell, there were already a few river cats swishing along, their whiskers trailing behind them.

Charlie wondered if Jimmy Mills had ever seen the fish's big brothers. He couldn't wait to see how the sad bastard would react. Probably piss himself without taking a breath.

"Here ya go."

Charlie made a good show out of jumping like he'd received the shock of his life. He even let out a gasp and jerked one hand up to his chest. He hoped it wasn't too obvious, but he had faith that Mills wasn't the sharpest knife in the drawer.

"Sorry 'bout that," Jimmy said. He slid a mostly-clean plate containing a hamburger that was only burned around the edges across the counter. "Enjoy, Charlie."

"You're not eating?" He pinched a morsel of beef from the burger and popped it into his mouth, giving Jimmy a smile as he chewed.

"Not really hungry."

"Still worried?"

"Nah."

"Jimmy, don't try to fuck with me."

The cook shrugged. "Sure. I'm still a little freaked. Why not? The fuckin' river's almost ten feet high!"

Charlie gave the storefront another glance. A discarded shoe drifted past the glass.

"More like eight, I think."

"Well, what the fuck ever! You ever seen something like this before?"

"Sure. I'm part of the river, remember?"

"So you're fucking with me now?"

"C'mon! I like to think you know me a little better than that. Fuckin' with you? That ain't gonna happen, Jimmy. Not when you're paying me to be here."

Mills appeared to calm down at the remark. He nodded slowly, his eyes hovering somewhere in the vicinity of the burger and fries.

"That mean you're trusting me again?"

"I guess so," Jimmy answered. "Not like I got a choice, right? We're stuck together for at least a few more days."

Charlie spun on his barstool until he was facing the tall glass storefront. He leaned back, resting his elbows on the lunch counter.

"Got that shit right, Jimmy. Nobody here but us." He felt the man stiffen behind him. Weird. He knew Mills was worried, but it almost felt like the guy was scared. He fought the urge to shrug. Let the man stew a bit. It was more than a little funny.

"Think I'm gonna head upstairs," Jimmy said. "Creeping me out down here."

"You still think the water's gonna get through?"

"I don't. I'm just . . . Shit, I don't know. Maybe. I don't like lookin' at the fucking river. That okay with you?"

"Sure thing, Jimmy. I'll just finish my burger. Might curl up in a booth and have myself a nap afterward. That okay?"

"Sure. Why wouldn't it be?"

He tore a bite off of the burger and chewed. Not bad. Not as dry as sawdust and tastier than your average lump of charcoal. Jimmy had really outdone himself.

He motioned at his throat with one hand. Mills read the gesture well, and a second later Charlie had a room temperature Coke sitting in front of him. He pulled a swig off the bottle and washed down the burger. He took another sip before speaking.

"Don't know. Maybe you need me to hold your hand some more?"

"You're a real asshole, Charlie. Know that?"

"Ever since my mama told me. Thanks for verifying it, though. Means a lot."

"Whatever." Jimmy left the dining room, grumbling under his breath. Nothing terribly original.

Charlie waited until he heard Mills's clunky footsteps on the stairs before stuffing another bite of hamburger into his mouth. Yeah, a nap would be good right about now. He didn't like that he'd dozed off. It wasn't a good sign. Maybe an hour of good sleep would keep him up, alert.

Hell, maybe his dreams would take a better turn.

Tammie looked into his eyes, and he saw love there. He saw sanity and eternity wrapped in a lover's embrace. He could spend the rest of his life with this woman, this beauty with black hair that fell to her shoulders and eyes like Absinthe. He could leave the craziness of Sulfer, the terror of his destiny.

She would save him.

They lay on a blanket on the banks of the Ohio. Their bodies lingered against each other. Slowly, their muscles relaxed as their lovemaking came to an end.

"What are you thinking?" she said. Her voice was a whisper that carried promises so beautiful they almost hurt.

"Thinkin' about you," he answered. "About us."

"And?"

"And I like thinkin' that way."

He climbed off of her sweat-slicked body and rested beside her. The old blanket felt too warm against his skin. It clung to him, dragged at him. The heat of July had spent the day punishing them both, and it wasn't so quick to let go.

But the heat had begun to retreat as the sun dipped below the horizon. Cool air began to dance through the tall grass that covered the sloped bank. It found the lovers and kissed their flesh. Charlie watched goosebumps rise on Tammie's arms and legs. He'd be ready again soon. He couldn't resist her beauty, hadn't been capable of such a feat since they'd met. If she wanted, he'd provide.

She smiled. "You are so full of shit, Charlie Crawford."

"That what you think?"

"You bet your ass it is."

"Now, why in hell—"

"Because you don't like thinkin'."

"What?"

"Your brain isn't the sunniest place, Charlie. We both know that's a fact. You got shadows up there, and you've always had 'em. They're always gonna be there. They're a part of you."

He nodded, but his eyes stayed locked on hers. "You ain't lying. I won't pretend for a second that you are. And you know what? Those shadows aren't going away anytime soon.

"You light 'em up a little, though. They're thinner when I think about you, and sometimes I can even ignore them for awhile."

She looked worried. "You shouldn't—"

"Doesn't matter."

"Yes it does, Charlie! You know how important you are. When it comes down, you'll need to be there. You have to be ready. You've known that your entire life."

"We all got parts to play, right. At least most of us do. I haven't forgotten, and I can't, not ever. Doesn't matter how hard I try. It just feels farther away when you're here. That's all. I think about you, and sometimes I even wonder if everything'll be okay in the end."

She gave him a grin. "You don't think it will?"

"How should I know? The end hasn't shown up yet."

He leaned in close and pressed his lips to hers. She breathed slow and sweet, her soft breeze teasing him. He felt her pull away, and every inch of him screamed in protest.

"Don't be so eager," she said. "You and me, we got all kinds of time."

"That we do," he answered. And he meant it. Something about Tammie calmed him even as it kicked his body into high gear. He could take his time with her, and he somehow knew it would all be okay. They had all the time in the world.

She pushed herself to her feet. Her pale skin caught the last of the day's light and glowed like a cooling ember. Charlie found himself struck.

"Where you going?" he asked. "You thinkin' about leaving me?"

"Not a bit." She turned and stepped toward the river. "I'll be back for you before you know it."

He watched her go. He admired her smooth skin and the way it moved with each step, pulling tight over muscle. So beautiful.

He smiled as she took her first confident steps into the Ohio.

Judging by Jimmy's screams, things had picked up nicely.

Charlie didn't bother jumping awake this time. He kept his shit far too together for something like that. Instead he took his time, letting out a good yawn and giving his limbs a quality stretch as he stood up from the booth. He probably should have been stiff as a board after catching a nap on the uncomfortable seat, but he was used to sleeping in awkward places.

Jimmy kept going off like some hillbilly fire alarm. Pigs died without making so much goddamn noise.

Charlie only half-wondered what had set off Mills. Could be anything, the guy was such a high-strung piece of work, but he figured there was something particular inspiring Jimmy to sing so well.

He rolled his shoulders and rocked his head back and forth. Couldn't be anything in the building setting Jimmy off—at least not so soon—so there had to be something in the street. Feeling good and ready to get a move on, he turned to the storefront and looked at the water flowing past the windows.

"Well, I'll be," he said. "Didn't take you long at all, did it?" He stepped forward and touched his hands to the glass. He gazed out at the thing in the street, and a smile that was mostly awe appeared on his lips.

"The others will be here soon, won't they? Not much time?"

He didn't wait for an answer, but instead walked to the diner's rear and started up the stairs. Might as well see how the bossman was doing. With any luck, the guy hadn't crapped himself.

Jimmy had stopped screaming, at least. Instead, he stood at the open windows, clinging to the frame with one white-knuckled hand and pointing down at the street with the other. His face was slack and pale, and he sucked in breath after breath with a rasping, croaking sound that made Charlie want to piss himself with laughter. This asshole was supposed to be a magician?

"Beauty, ain't she?"

"It's--" He fell back into his breathing again.

"What's the matter, Jimmy?" Charlie asked as he started across the floor. The second story of Jimmy's building was a single loft with a high ceiling. A few boxes had been stacked near the back, but the rest was empty save a coat of chipped paint and a growing supply of dust and cobwebs. The wooden floor creaked under Charlie's feet, but it was solid as a tank. Just about everything in town was, even the buildings that were falling apart.

When he reached his temporary employer, he slapped a hand against the man's shoulder. Jimmy let out a scream and almost jumped out the window.

"You never see a catfish before, Jimmy?"

The man's eyes widened in a way about as close to comical as you could get and still be pathetic.

"Catfish?"

"Sure. What did you think it was?"

"That's a catfish?"

"You didn't listen to that last sentence at all, did ya?"

Jimmy thrust his finger down at the water. "That fuckin' thing down there's a goddamn monster, Charlie! It ain't no catfish!"

Charlie looked down at the creature. Just over ten feet long and probably a good five feet wide. Dull gray with muddy brown splotches. Its whiskers drifted back four feet or more on either side, and the thing's tail looked like it could gut a man like Jimmy. The fish wasn't trying to get anywhere. The journey onto Second Street had probably tuckered out the poor bastard enough. Still, its tail swished back and forth lazily. Its gills pumped in and out like bellows, marking time since well before the founding of Sulfer.

What a beautiful fucking thing.

"That, my friend, is one helluva catfish. Bottom dweller. They found a whole ton of 'em down past Rising Sun when they were building Markland Dam. You hardly ever see 'em up from the mud and such, but these are special times, Jimmy. Special times, indeed. Now, don't be such a little girl."

"They found a ton of 'em?"

Jimmy's mouth wasn't closing, like it was broke or something. Charlie fought the urge to stick his finger in the gaping hole.

"Well, that one down there might be a ton for all I know. Heard there's some even bigger, and I don't doubt it for a second. The Ohio's got some real fucked up shit in her." He fought hard to keep the shadows from his expression as he spoke.

"But there was more than one?" True to form, the man's jaw remained slack.

143

"Dozens, at least. Look, Jimmy. You've spent most of your life in Sulfer, so you're supposed to not get freaked out by this sort of thing. Something spooking ya?"

Mills shook his head a little too fast. "Naw, Charlie. Fuck you; there ain't nothin'."

"Good to hear. The important thing, though, is you gotta get your shit together, and I mean fast. That big bitch down there is just the beginning of what this flood's gonna bring up from the mud and muck. Now, I've got a few of my tricks up, and they should keep us plenty safe, but there's some shit I can't prepare for. Some stuff you just gotta deal with as it comes. I'll need your help, because you're not some fly by night trickster, man. You been at magic for awhile, too, and you can help me out."

Jimmy's face had turned from white to a color resembling old cheese. Or maybe old Cheetos.

"What's coming?"

"Let me ask you something, Jimmy. What's the weirdest shit you've ever seen?"

The man answered without thinking. "The time Deena Simms gave birth to a cat. That was pretty fucked up."

"Well, she was five at the time. That's the strangest thing, though?"

"Yeah."

Charlie looked down at the water-filled street. The giant catfish had started moving again, its tail swinging back and forth like a club. Water moved out of its way as if it were scared of the big fish. The cat charged away with surprising speed, its body disappearing beneath the muck after only a second or two.

"Gotta tell ya, Jimmy . . . "

"What?"

"We could be in for a rough couple of days."

She moved with the grace of a goddess, knifing clean and crisp through the water. The rippling sounds of her body in the Ohio filled the valley. Even the summer crickets fell silent to listen to her symphony.

Charlie leaned back on his elbows and watched her through the swaying grass. The moon had risen into the sky, and its light cast silver daggers over the water. Tammie's skin became a gliding ray of light, beautiful and awe-inspiring.

He chuckled. He wasn't used to such thoughts, and they struck him as more than a little ridiculous. They were true, though. Every idea that floated through his mind did so honestly. There was no irony, none of his usual sarcasm. There was just pure love and desire for a woman who made him feel good about a world gone sour.

"You laughing at me?" she called from the river. Her words carried a smile.

Charlie climbed to his feet. She had stopped swimming. Instead, she waded about thirty feet out, her head bobbing up and down on top of the river.

He grinned as he called out to her. "Far from it!"

"My ass!"

That did kick a guffaw out of him.

"I knew it!" Her voice remained playful.

"You know no such thing! Can't you tell when a man's laughin' at himself?"

Her own giggles cut through the air. "Not when I'm busy laughing at him!"

"Oh, that's just mean! You're gonna get yours when you come outta that river!"

"Charlie Crawford! You gonna make me wait?"

He stepped forward, and grass scraped across his naked thighs. "You don't want me coming in there after ya!"

"Why's that? You such a bad swimmer you don't want me saving ya?"

"Oh, that is it!" He started down the bank faster. He heard Tammie laugh good and loud. The sound echoed along the river. He picked up speed and broke through the clinging grass, ignored the rocks and bottle caps that cut at his feet. All he cared about was Tammie. Nothing else mattered but the woman in the river.

"Hope you're ready!" he said as water splashed over his feet. "This is gonna hurt you a lot more than it hurts me!"

He expected a taunt in reply. Instead, Tammie screamed.

Charlie sat at the lunch counter again, screwing a Marlboro into his lips and offering one to Jimmy. Mills took one with shaking fingers and failed to light the fucker on the first four tries.

Charlie shook his head and blew a plume at the ceiling.

"What do you know about the big flood, Jimmy?"

"You mean like the biblical one?"

"No. I mean like the one in 1913. The one that happened here."

"I think I've heard of it."

"And what did you hear?"

"Water. Lots of it."

"Shit, that barely scratches the surface. Everything was covered up to Fourth Street. I don't mean just a little bit of water, either. I mean a full story, at least. Not as bad as this, though."

"We're at a full story now, Charlie."

"Nope. We're at two." Charlie took another puff and watched the other half of his conversation through a screen of smoke.

Jimmy didn't respond. Big shocker, that.

"How many basements you got, Jimmy? One or two?"

"One," Mills said in a tone that sounded pissed off and stupid at the same time.

"Then you're sitting on a grave, buddy."

"What?"

"You love the shit out of that word, don't ya?"

"Fuck you."

Charlie stubbed out his smoke on the countertop and lit a new one.

"Here's the deal. You can look it up at the library when the town dries out, if you don't believe me.

"Sulfer used to be ten feet lower than it is now. Back in 1913, the Ohio spilled her guts all over the town and sat there, ten feet high and pissed to the goddamn gills, for close to two weeks. Town had never seen anything like it. Worst part is that not a soul saw it coming, either. Word says Tommy Baker's grandfather did it trying to summon something out of the river. Succeeded, too. Lot of folks lost their lives, though, so ruined furniture wasn't the only thing left behind to clean up once the water went back down. Lotta bodies to pack up, too.

"So the folks left behind--and there was more than a few, not like the flood took everybody--were stuck with one bitch of a job. They had to clean up a town that had basically lost the lower ten feet of everything, and they had a whole fuck-ton of corpses to get rid of on top of it all. So, they got to work. They piled bodies in as many basements as they could and sealed them shut. They used a few cantrips and whatnot to preserve the bodies, make sure they didn't start smelling. All the garbage they threw out in the street as fill. Once they were ready, they paved over everything and rebuilt the storefronts. Boom. Whole new town of Sulfer."

"You're shittin' me," Jimmy managed to say after half a minute of dumb silence.

"I look like I'm shittin' you?"

"You wanna know the truth, Charlie? I can't even tell."

"Then I guess you'll have to wait and see, Jimmy. Don't know how plain I can make it to ya."

Mills shook his head. "You're fuckin' with me, Charlie. Don't try to tell me different. I get it, okay? You got me stuck in here, and there ain't a place I can go. Great time to pick on Jimmy Mills, right? See how scared you can get me, then tell everybody down at Hilljack's about it on dollar draft night."

Charlie pulled a drag off his Marlboro, letting Jimmy finish his thought.

"Well, fuck you, Charlie Crawford. I'm paying your ass to help keep my place of business in pristine working order, so you don't get to pull shit on me. You're here until I decide you can piss off, and then what are you gonna do? Huh? You think you can swim your miserable ass all the way to dry land?"

"You want to end our partnership, Mr. Mills?"

"Maybe I do!"

Charlie ran the fingers of one hand through his hair before fixing his eyes on Jimmy again. "You want me to go, I'll go. Let me grab my shit."

"You didn't bring anything."

"Then I guess I won't have much to carry." He got up from the lunch counter and stepped past Jimmy, not even bothering to give the bastard a glance. He moved toward the kitchen, stepping with purpose.

"How you even gonna get out of here?" Jimmy asked.

"Got my ways. You oughta know me better than that."

"But there's giant catfish out there!"

"And if I was a pussy like you, that might mean half a fuck to me. Have fun, Jimmy. Try not to piss yourself while I'm gone."

He counted his ringing footsteps against the linoleum as he pushed through the swinging doors into the kitchen. He reached the five before Jimmy stopped him.

"Wait up, Charlie."

Crawdad gave himself another one of those winning smiles. "Yeah?"

"Look, man. I'm sorry, okay? Just a little freaked out. Stick around, and let's ride this out."

He turned to face Jimmy. "Gonna cost you two hundred more."

"What?"

"I don't like being insulted. You can agree to it, or I can go."

"Fine. Shit on me."

"I don't think there'll be call for that."

Charlie dashed into the river like a madman, a desperate buffoon. Water flew in every direction as his feet kicked. Even as he fell waist-deep into the muddy current, when he should have known to dive and swim, he kept trying to run. His panicked brain refused to deliver any other commands. Run. Save her. Everything else was white noise and Tammie's screams.

She'd gone under several times. She hadn't sunk, but been jerked violently beneath the surface. She'd managed to claw her way back, but it took longer each time, and her screaming had to be stealing far too much of her strength.

"Tammie!" He couldn't think of anything else to say. The short circuits in his mind hissed curses at him, refusing to think of any spells or tricks that might help his lover. His thoughts cleared just enough to let him dive forward. His body knifed though the water, and he came up kicking, paddling, swimming with everything he could muster.

He'd last seen her no more than thirty feet from the shore. Still, it felt like miles before he saw her fingertips clawing at the river's surface. The tiny splashes they made terrified him. How long had it been since she last came up?

He reached for Tammie's hand, and something jerked it away. Her fingertips disappeared into the depths, leaving behind rippling blackness. He stared in horror for a split second and then his brain finally kicked in, telling him what to do.

The words to the protection spell crossed his lips in the instant before he dove underwater. It wasn't a powerful spell, but Tammie could die in the length of time it would take him to perform something better.

He hoped he had enough breath left in his lungs. He'd need every last bit of it.

He searched the water with his hands, his eyes useless. He felt currents thick with terror. He followed them, kicking madly, reaching, and his fingers brushed flesh he recognized as Tammie's.

He shot forward and grabbed her fully. He clenched his fingers around her wrists and held on with everything he had. Something pulled them both down, something strong. He kicked against it, but it provided no resistance. A scream of frustration raced up from his lungs, but he bit it back. He needed that air.

How long had it been since Tammie's last breath? How long before she was gone?

Squeezing his eyes shut against the Ohio's polluted waters, he swung his legs down and wrapped them tight around Tammie's waist. He felt her stop fighting. She knew it was him. He almost smiled. She'd recognized his touch.

He had one shot, and he knew it. He mustered all of his concentration, ignoring the water that rushed past as they were dragged down. Instead, he found the words he needed, and he spoke them.

They came out as a garbled, bubbling mess, but their intent was clear. His magic worked.

His energy shoved through the water around him, blasting everything that wasn't him, wasn't Tammie. He felt the river shudder, and suddenly they weren't sinking anymore. They floated slowly upward. He started kicking, holding on to his lover with his hands. He felt weak, spent from the magic, but he fought the water for every inch. He didn't know if Tammie helped, but he hoped. Without her aid, the thing that had grabbed her might catch them once more.

They broke the surface just as his lungs threatened to give in. Cold night air slapped his face, and he fully realized he was still alive.

"You okay?" he asked.

She coughed, sputtering water past her lips. Her eyes were wide and frightened, and he took that as a sign she was still among the living.

He paddled toward shore, dragging Tammie alongside him.

"You're not shittin' me, right? You wouldn't do that, would ya? Not now."

Charlie shook his head. He'd sat in silence, looking down at the flooded street, for almost an hour. Jimmy had paced behind him the entire time, feet clip-clopping on the wooden floor and hands wringing so hard they sounded like stretching rubber bands. Charlie did his best to stay focused through the long piece of time. Strong odds said they'd have to deal with some serious shit before all was said and done, and the fact of the matter was he didn't know if he was ready for all of it just yet.

He had a job to do, though. Sooner or later he'd have to swallow his fear and do it.

Something broke the surface of the water below, then disappeared. Charlie watched the rippling spot left behind on the water's surface, but he couldn't find any clue that might tell him what had caused the disturbance. He wondered if Mills had seen it. The guy wasn't screaming, so more likely he hadn't.

"Charlie?"

"I'm gonna need salt."

A moment of silence, then, "Huh?"

"Salt, Jimmy. Your customers put it on their fries. I need some. How much do you have?"

"You want packets."

He sighed. "If that's all you have. Can you do better than that?"

"Gotta tin. Use it to fill up the shakers."

"That'll do. Where's it at?"

"Dry storage. Next to the walk-in."

"Good." He climbed to his feet. He used both hands to brush the dust off his ass, then looked to the sky and saw the first tinges of orange and gold that meant a sunset. "You better get some sleep, okay? It's getting late."

"You serious?"

"Yeah. I'm all kinds of serious. What? You don't want to sleep?"

"I didn't say that."

"Then if I were you I'd shut my eyes and start sawing some logs, Jimmy."

"What are you gonna do?"

One last glance at the street below. It wasn't quite time.

"Whatever I can."

Her breath returned by the time they reached the shore. Charlie helped her out of the shallows, his arm wrapped around her shoulders. She looked okay. Terrified, but okay.

"*Tammie, are you still in there?*"

153

She nodded, and he'd never been so thankful for such a simple motion. He released a long, relieved breath.

"What was it?" she asked.

He began to speak and then his jaw snapped shut. He didn't know. He hadn't seen Tammie's attacker, hadn't felt it. He only knew it was strong. It could have been anything from the big river cats to a vampire using the muddy water to hide from the sun.

"Charlie?"

He shook his head clear. "Yeah."

"My ankle's cold."

He tore his eyes from her face long enough to glance at her ankle. What he saw there held his gaze. Whatever had attacked Tammie had scratched her leg to hell and back. He counted five deep gouges in the skin and muscle beneath her calf.

"Oh, hell." The words escaped before he could stop them. He looked to Tammie's eyes and saw new fear there.

"What is it?"

"A scratch. Don't worry." He hoped he sounded convincing, but he doubted his abilities.

The cuts should have been bleeding heavily. They were deep enough to hit all kinds of blood vessels. Tammie's leg was clean, though. Instead of blood, water seeped from the gouges. It traveled down her ankle and around to her heel, where it dripped into the grass of the riverbank.

Charlie tried to keep his breathing steady as he inspected the cuts more closely. The torn skin surrounding each wound was a dark blue that blanched to pure white farther from the cut.

He'd never seen anything like it, and that frightened him.

"Charlie?" Her voice wavered, barely restrained horror pushing it up and down, left and right.

"It's fine," he said. "Let's get you dressed and home, okay? Enough fun for one night."

She laughed the slightest bit. "Yeah. Okay."

Slowly, he helped her to her feet.

"That really gonna help?"

Jimmy's voice almost sounded bored, like he had convinced himself this was all some big prank and Charlie was just playing a part. There was still an edge to it, though. A little waver that said everything that needed saying.

Charlie sighed as he grabbed another fistful of salt from the tin and extended his arm over the water. He let the mineral sift through his fingers, falling to the flooded street. "It should," he said. "Current's not too strong. Should settle pretty good. Guess we'll have to wait and see."

"Doesn't salt dissolve in water?"

Charlie blinked. "Not when I put it there."

"So what's coming? We need to get weapons or something?" Good. Jimmy believed him.

"Weapons? Like what?"

Jimmy shrugged. "I got knives and shit down in the kitchen."

"Doesn't hurt, I guess," Charlie replied. "Don't really think it'll do a lot of good, though."

"Why not?"

Charlie took a single step away from the window. He looked to the sky. The gold and orange were gone.

The red had darkened, and a purple hue had crept around its edges. Night was coming on fast.

"Because I don't know what's coming," he answered. He sprinkled a thick line of salt along the window's ledge, which was painfully close to the floor. Even worse, it was only about four feet up from the water line.

"You don't know?"

"Not really. Could be something real bad. Hell, Jimmy, it might not be anything at all. I'm betting it's a little worse than a giant catfish, though."

"But you don't know? And you think it might come in here?"

"I think it might try. I'm gonna shut the windows up tight just in case, and I'm hoping the salt will stop anything getting through, but there's some terrible shit in that river. Sure as hell, there's stuff I don't want to look in the eye."

Jimmy stood at the edge of a long shadow. He shivered the slightest bit, his eyes fixed on Charlie. "Stuff like what?"

"I don't know, Jimmy. I thought I'd just got done tellin' you that." He swung the windows shut and locked them. Once they were good and tight, he placed a hand to each pane and muttered a simple charm. It might work; it might not. Time would tell. "And don't give me that 'the river's part of me' shit. It don't add up to jack or shit at the end of the day."

"But--"

"You've seen the stairs, right?"

Jimmy nodded.

"That's what I thought."

Of course Jimmy had. Everybody in Sulfer knew about the goddamn stairs. A series of concrete slabs, ten feet by ten. They started at the edge of State Road 56--the two-lane blacktopper that ran between Sulfer and Rising Sun--at the mouth of Third Street and ran all the way into the Ohio's syrupy waters. Not a single resident of Sulfer remembered a time when the slabs hadn't been there. *Older than the town,* most said. Just about everybody figured the concrete served as a set of steps for something in the river. Nobody knew what that something might be, though. They only knew it had to be something big.

Mills's face had gone more than a little pale. "You think whatever needs the stairs--"

"I doubt it. I'm just using it as an example of what might be coming, okay? What <u>could</u> decide to haul ass into town. Like I said before, it could be anything that comes or it could be nothing. Now go and get those knives, you think they'll make you feel any better."

"Sure." Jimmy nodded a little too eagerly, then raced for the wooden steps at the loft's rear.

He returned his gaze to the window. The sun was officially gone, and night had made her big debut. The storm that caused the flood had occurred five days before and well upriver, leaving the night sky clear. Stars and a half moon shone down on the town, giving Charlie just enough light to appraise the buildings on the other side of Second Street. They were dark, but who could tell if they were deserted or not? Could be folks inside who'd stuck around to protect their interests. The upper stories might also be full of creepers. The bastards were just a human form of vermin, clawing for any scratch of a living they could make. You couldn't shake the bastards once you were flush with them--worse than cockroaches and rats put together and bred for show. Damned amazing Mills didn't have a crop in the loft. Not that Charlie would be able to spot a creeper that didn't want to be seen. The buggers could dig in like ticks on a basset hound if they had half a mind to.

Maybe whatever was coming wouldn't spot them. Right. Like it would ignore what was probably dozens of bodies buried beneath the building. Charlie cursed himself. He could kill himself for not making sure he wasn't walking into one of the graves. He'd let personal reasons drag him into this one, and now he was stuck on what might well be a pile of bait.

Yeah, he needed some bait, but had something real specific in mind...

He heard the proprietor's footsteps loud and clomping on the stairs at the rear of the loft. Sounded like a sasquatch trying to sneak up to the second floor.

"Picture of grace, aren't you?"

"What?" Jimmy replied. He really did have a fondness for that word.

"Nevermind, okay? What did you get?"

"I thought I was getting knives."

"So did I. Did you?"

"Yeah." The cook held out a butcher knife, presenting the handle to Charlie.

The blade was probably eight inches long, and it gleamed even in the faint starlight. Not bad. Would probably cut a bastard up good and proper before it even thought about going dull.

"You got one for yourself?"

"Not exactly." Jimmy raised one arm and presented the meat cleaver he held in that hand. If the knife he'd given Charlie was dangerous, then this piece of hardware looked like an atomic bomb.

Cooks and butchers, man. Creepy, dangerous fuckers. Charlie eyed the blade and couldn't help but whisper his thanks that he wasn't waiting out the flood with Davey Ross, the butcher down at Tandy's. He'd seen the way Davey liked to smile when cutting up meat, and it was enough to put a sharp stab of fear in any man, even somebody like him.

"Jesus Christ, Jimmy."

"You said it might be something bad."

"Yeah, and I didn't expect the mad chopping prick of Sulfer to come marching back up the stairs, either."

"You want the knife or not?"

"Oh, I want it! Mostly in case you come at me with your fuckin' man-hacker there!"

Anger flashed across Jimmy's face like a racing shadow. "Oh, fuck you! How about you leave now?"

"At dark? Nice try, but that ain't gonna happen. Sorry about your trouble." He held Jimmy's eyes for a long time, until the darkness of night threatened to swallow them both.

Mills looked at their surroundings. From his expression, he appeared to be noticing the shadows for the first time.

"Maybe we should make some light."

"Right," Charlie said. "Maybe I should open the windows back up and put out a sign that says 'Free Crackers. Get 'em while they're hot.'"

"Think light'll give us away?"

"I'm pretty sure that's what I meant, yeah."

Jimmy's mouth twisted with the first signs of more bitching, then went slack as a scraping sound filled the cavernous loft.

Crawford's muscles locked for a split second, then did something that wasn't quite the same as relaxing. He heard the noise, and he knew it was anything but good. Slowly, he turned to face the wall of windows. He wished he'd find a brick wall--anything solid--but wishing wasn't going to do a damn bit of good in this situation. He cast the thought away--better to forget about it and move on than keep wishing while you were ripped to shreds.

The sound was slow, ominous. Charlie didn't know if it was made by a set of nails or claws. A sudden image of cuts that dripped water flashed through his head, and he forced it down. Too soon.

He could tell by the sound that something was feeling its way, testing the path. The cautious exploratory nature worried him. It meant whatever was making the noise was at least a little smart. Maybe it would be intelligent enough to stay away, to feel the salt and hexes that were meant to keep such awful things at bay.

But if it was working its way up the building, then it was in the water he'd salted. That wasn't a good sign.

Jimmy reached out and touched his shoulder. "What do--"

Charlie placed a finger to his lips, and somehow Jimmy managed to understand what that meant. Good boy.

He backed up a step, raising the knife to his waist. He felt Jimmy shiver at his side, and he hoped the guy wouldn't get freaked and start swinging that cleaver around like a panicked madman.

He hoped whatever was outside would go away.

Tough luck.

The sound of even more claws scratching on the brick outside made that hope evaporate like corn whiskey on a sunny day. Charlie heard at least three sets on the building now, each one reaching, scraping. The noise was terrible even in its relative softness. It was just so persistent. Whatever these things were, they sure didn't look to be going anywhere, and that wasn't a damn bit of good.

"Where's the salt?" he whispered.

From the corner of his eye, he saw Jimmy point. He followed the man's outstretched finger--shaking as it was--and found the canister. He'd left it next to the window.

Way to fuckin' go, Charlie.

He didn't know if the salt would really help, but he knew he'd feel a lot better with it in his posession. What was on the other side of that window? He knew it wasn't the main event, but it could wind up being one hell of an undercard brawler. Did he really want to risk finding out?

He thought it over for an instant and decided no, not really.

"Jimmy, go grab the salt."

He could almost hear the tendons in Jimmy's neck creak as the man turned to face him. "Are you out of your fuckin' mind?" the cook said.

"We're gonna need that salt."

"Then you go get it. Last I checked, I'm the guy paying you."

Charlie let out an annoyed breath. "Fine." He took a step forward, and the creaking of his foot on the floorboards sent a shiver from his toes up to the top of his cranium. His breath whispered past his lips-- sounding impossibly loud to his ears. *Bullshit,* he told himself. *Letting your mind play those familiar tricks. You're better than that, Charlie.*

He could push them back. He knew just the spell, had used it a time or two in the past. He needed to save his energy, though. There were other things out there, and he'd need all of his mojo to confront them.

So he took a second step, followed by a third. His eyes never left the window as he moved forward. He kept a steady pace, and he forced the nerves that jangled throughout his body to settle the hell down and do what they were told. He knew the body was a simple instrument, just like the mind. You could play it any way you wanted, if you knew how. He slowed his breath, which slowed his heart. His arms began to swing in a way that was casual and sure. Hell, just walking across the floor to pick up some salt. Didn't matter that there might be some goddamn river monstrosity on the other side, just waiting to get inside and take a bite out of old Charlie Crawdad. Nope. Didn't matter for squat. All that mattered was his leisurely walk to scoop up his old friend Mr. Salt Tin.

Just a few more feet. No big deal.

Charlie eyed the salt, and in the same instant he heard the squealing sound of something scratching at the windowpane. It sounded like a cat dying on a quiet night—squalling with pain and rage. His controlled breath and pulse jumped right into the stratosphere. *Fuck you, buddy! How dare you try to keep us in check?*

Charlie felt his eyes begin to slide toward the sound, and he commanded them to stop right the fuck where they were. He didn't know what was scraping at the glass only five feet to his left, but he was sure he didn't care to find out until he was at least a little farther away. Behind him, Jimmy hit a screeching note that almost matched the scratching at the pane. Good for him.

Charlie stooped and stretched out a single arm, snatching up the canister of salt with grateful fingers.

"There we are!"

And a single pane of glass shattered inward.

Charlie leaped away from the window, and he was only dimly aware of the sound of tinkling glass as it hit the floor. This time he allowed himself to look at the noise. His eyes fixed on the busted window as he fumbled the top off of the tin.

The hand that appeared in the broken window didn't sport any scales, and Charlie took that as a bit of a comfort. The skin was blacker than expensive ink. Its three fingers and thumb ended with long, curved talons that shone a pale yellow in the starlight. He'd never seen anything like it, and that was saying something. He only knew it wasn't the creature that had attacked Tammie. It was a small relief, but he still wasn't too keen on examining the rest of the creature.

"Sweet Jesus," he whispered as he scooped a handful of salt from the tin. "Don't let this be bullshit." He darted forward and threw the mineral. It flew through the air like a speeding cloud, coating the hand with a fine layer.

The skin began to smoke at once.

"Hurts a might, don't it?" Charlie said as he watched the hand bubble and burn. The fingers peeled away from the window all at once, and a cry like a broken police siren filled the air.

Charlie turned to Jimmy and flashed him a smile. Mills replied by raising the cleaver over his shoulder, cocking his arm back like a Triple A pitcher.

"You fuckin' crazy?" Charlie screamed. He flinched as the cleaver left Jimmy's swinging arm and cartwheeled through the air. He heard the continuous chop of the blade, so loud it was audible over the howling creature on the other side of the window. He tucked the tin of salt close to his chest and dove out of the cleaver's path.

He crashed to the floor like he'd been suplexed by Ricky Dalton, who made extra cash on the weekends as a wrestler down in Louisville named Rugged Ricky Danger. In the same instant, he heard the cleaver's blade strike home in something thick and meaty. The monster's cry fell silent at once.

He looked up from the floor to see a hideous face in the window. It was black and smooth, glistening with a thin sheen of river water. Narrow eyes that were milky white broke up the darkness. A large mandible full of dagger-like teeth hung in two sections, but Charlie couldn't tell if it was meant to function that way or not. The cleaver's blade bisected the face perfectly, and light from the stars and moon shimmered off the visible steel. The monster held onto the window an instant longer, then fell back into the water.

Charlie's gaze shifted to Jimmy.

The cook stood frozen, his eyes locked on the now empty window. The air was silent save the dying waves from the creature's splashdown. Mills didn't appear to care, though. He wasn't taking his eyes off that window.

"Jimmy?"

"Yeah?"

"How the fuck did you do that?"

"That thing, it was still coming in."

"Well, I know that now."

"I just saw its face and threw."

"And a good fucking shot, too. Jesus, man! They teach that shit in the crap-ass school where you learned to burn burgers?"

"Fuck you, Crawdad. Your precious little salt didn't stop it!"

Charlie climbed to his feet and used his free hand to dust off his knees one at a time.

"Maybe not. Hurt the fuck out of it, though! That earn me any points, or are ya just gonna throw something else in my direction?"

"What the hell was that thing?"

Charlie shrugged. "Beats me, man. I've seen more than snapping turtles come out of the river, but that's a new one on me."

"You think there'll be more?"

He stopped and listened. Silence greeted him, and he was thankful for it. "Don't think so. You probably gave 'em something to think about with your little axe-throwing act."

Jimmy turned away, heading for the stairs. "Hope so," he said.

"Hey, Jimmy!"

The cook turned around. "Yeah?"

"Seriously, where the fuck did you learn to throw like that?"

He blinked. "I didn't. Just saw that thing and panicked." He walked the rest of the way to the narrow steps and started down.

Charlie watched Mills's shadow stretch and then finally disappear. A shaft of flickering yellow light spilled up the stairs from the kitchen, and he watched that light for a long while before following Jimmy downstairs.

Almost time.

She grew worse fast, her health diving from fine to not so good to downright terrible in less than a day.

By the time Charlie drove her back to her parents house, she had begun to sweat. Perspiration poured from her skin as if somebody had left a tap running. She looked feverish, but her temperature had dropped. Where her eyes should have been red and rheumy, they grew sunken and ringed with pale blue. Every vein grew darker and closer to the skin. The wounds on her ankle pruned, the flesh there soaked through and beginning to chafe.

Charlie laid her on her bed. Her room still looked like it belonged to a teenager, right down to the pink and purple bedspread that was immediately soaked with sweat that smelled the slightest bit like mud and fish.

"Darling, you're twenty years old," he said through a worried smile. "Time to redecorate."

She still lived at home. Her parents were gone, visiting relatives in Indianapolis. It was the only reason he'd been able to sneak her out of the house and down to the river in the first place. *Dammit, why did they have to be gone? Who the fuck went to Indianapolis for any reason?*

"I feel wrong, Charlie."

"You still look great. Better than a porn star."

"Shut up."

He nodded, giving her a smile that felt as fake as it probably looked. She returned the smile and closed her eyes.

Charlie got to work. Over the following hours he tried every chant and remedy he could think of. He stuffed her wounds with salt, ash, and clover, but she kept right on leaking. Her body grew thinner and thinner, the rest of her skin turning blue and milk white, shrinking over her bones. The room filled with the think scent of the Ohio.

Charlie threw things. Broke things. Neither helped him feel any better. Neither gave him an answer.

Hours later, he barely recognized Tammie. She was a waterlogged shadow of blue and white. Her eyes had taken on a milky hue. They bugged out of their sockets slightly, and he knew they were filling with fluid, swelling. He ran his fingers through her hair, and it fell out in clumps that turned to river water almost immediately.

He swallowed hard. "Tammie?"

She rasped something, maybe his name. She tried again, and the words gurgled deep in her throat. She coughed violently before she managed to draw another breath.

"Don't talk," he said. "Just don't even try. I just want to say I'm sorry. I love you, and I'm sorry.

"I'm sorry I couldn't save you."

He knelt on the soaked carpet and began to cry.

167

* * *

More than twelve hours later, the sunlight had arrived to pierce the green water that flooded Second Street. The waters would crest before nightfall. They'd begin to recede before the next sunrise.

Charlie Crawford sat in a booth, eyes locked on the table in front of him. His mind was heavy.

He didn't have much time left.

"It's amazing, isn't it?" Jimmy's voice was almost childlike. It snapped Charlie out of his deeper thoughts.

"What do you mean?" Crawford asked.

"The river," Jimmy answered. His hands were pressed to the glass, and his eyes remained fixed on the window, watching as something that looked like a squid made of steel squirmed past the storefront. "So much crazy stuff in it. Blows your mind."

"You come a long way from being scared of a catfish."

"Maybe. Guess I just saw the light. Guy's allowed to do that, right?"

"The light? You know better than that, Jimmy. Ain't no light but the sun. It's all darkness past that. Heaven ain't shit but a myth the devil's scared of."

Mills shook his head, dismissive. "Says you."

"Says everything. Entire world only makes sense when you take God out of it. Otherwise, you gotta rely on that 'mysterious ways' bullshit, and that ain't done nobody a lick of good but teach 'em self-pity."

"Maybe. Still amazing, though."

"Wasn't little more than twelve hours ago you were pissin' yourself over what might be in the big green bitch. Then you kill something out of it, and you're both hunky and dory. Can't say I get that, Mr. Mills."

"Maybe there's nothing there for you to get, Charlie."

"Guess that's possible. It's rarely the case, though."

"You so sure?"

"Always am. It's how I keep my ticker clicking."

"That just makes you cocky."

"That makes me alive."

"Does it?" Jimmy turned to give him a look.

He flashed a smile in response. "I'm here, aren't I?"

Mills shrugged. "Until the water goes away, I guess."

"Well, we'll all be sad when that happens."

"Will we, now?"

He dropped his eyes to the tabletop for a moment, then met Jimmy's gaze and grinned.

"Fuck no, shit splat. I can't stand ya."

Mills turned away from the window, his hands clenching into fists for an instant before relaxing again. He managed to push the anger away from his face, but couldn't quite keep it out of his eyes. It churned there like black bile. It made the smile on his lips ring hollow, like the promise of a pretty woman or a young politician.

"Right," Jimmy said. "Screw yourself, Charlie Crawdad. I'm gonna grab some shut-eye. You should do the same."

Charlie shrugged and crawled out of the booth. He held his hands up in surrender as he approached Mills.

"Look, Jimmy. I'm sorry, okay? Seriously. You handled yourself real well last night, and you saved my goddamn skin. I'm not used to anybody pulling my bacon out of the fire but me, and I guess I just let it crank up my asshole-dial. So I'm sorry. And thank you." He held out a hand.

Jimmy looked deep into his eyes, and Charlie could tell he was searching for a lie. A moment later he took the hand and shook it.

"Anytime, Charlie."

"Glad to hear it."

Jimmy let go and walked past Charlie, heading for the back.

"Hey, Mills!"

"Yeah?" He turned to see what Charlie wanted.

Charlie threw the right with everything he hand, and Jimmy hit the deck like his switch had been flipped.

He stared at the soaked bed for a long time. Every last trace of Tammie was gone. The smell of mud and the squish of water in the carpet served as her corpse. Her belongings had become her grave marker.

He had called her parents. They were on their way back from Indy. He'd have to explain. If the conversation didn't kill him, Tammie's parents might.

Good. He probably deserved it.

He curled into a tight ball and sank deeper into her waterlogged bed.

Charlie was glad to see Jimmy remain out unconscious for so long. It gave him time to go upstairs and prepare. He bound the cook's wrists and ankles with duct tape before anything else. Last thing he needed was the guy coming to and raising a stink. One day earlier, he might not mind, but now he'd seen Mills lob a cleaver like a Cy Young winner, and he didn't want his head to wind up a strike zone.

Once he finished in the attic, was sure everything was just as he needed it, he checked in on Jimmy. The man was still out, even snoring a little. He almost laughed, but instead grabbed him under the arms and dragged him upstairs. He used thick loops of the silver tape to bind Jimmy's knees, then used a quick holding spell just to be sure he didn't squirm away. Once done, he took a satisfied breath. Mills wasn't going anywhere.

He tore the man's shirt off, and still Jimmy didn't snap out of it. Only when he took the knife and started carving the first symbol into Mills's chest did the man jolt awake with a scream.

"Whoa there, buddy," he said.

Jimmy let loose with another wail, his pain bouncing off the high ceiling. The spell kept him rooted to the floor, not that Charlie doubted it would.

"What the fuck are you doing to me?" Terror and pain shifted the pitch of Jimmy's voice an octave higher than normal.

"It's nothing personal. I'm using you. That's all." He dug the blade into flesh again, carving a smooth line along the sternum. Jimmy let out another scream before speaking.

"You *bastard!*"

"Never claimed to be anything different. Now try to shut up. I'm working."

"Fuck you!"

"Heard that one before. Try something new."

He finished the line and started another. Blood flowed freely down Mills's chest, tracing lines between his ribs and beginning to pool on the wooden floor. He wondered how messy it would be before he finished, decided he didn't really give a rat's ass.

Jimmy's scream became a roar. "I'm going to *kill* you for this, god*dammit!*"

"Heard that one, too. Hell, heard it just last week. It would be awful nice if you at least tried to make this entertaining. We're gonna be here a long time, and the last thing I want to do is fall asleep 'cause you're boring me to death."

The man's screams filled the dusty space. They echoed and circled and cracked. Charlie wondered if anybody was left in town to hear them, but he shrugged off the thought. It didn't matter. If anybody heard, they'd ignore it, same as always. Besides, he had work to do and only a few more hours to do it. The sun was past its zenith and heading downward. He had to be ready by nightfall. No point in wasting time with bullshit concerns.

Another line, this one crossing the other two. Spittle sprayed from between Mills's clenched teeth.

"Why you doing this, Charlie? Why the fuck you doing this to me?"

Charlie shook his head. "I figured you'd ask that, Jimmy. Didn't figure it would be so soon. Got miles to go before sunset, y'know?"

"Tell me!"

Figured. If Jimmy was anything, he was tenacious in his desire to have every single fucking thing explained to him. Fucking baby.

"Fine. You want answers, I'll fork 'em over. Almost twenty years ago, I lost somebody precious, somebody I loved."

Mills squeezed his eyes shut, pain burning across his features. "Tammie Bowers?"

"Got it in one. Something in the river attacked her, something I couldn't see. I got to her, but there was nothing I could do but watch her go. That's what I did, too. I watched until there wasn't a damn thing left. You shouldn't have to do that, nobody should. I tell ya, I've seen some awful shit, but that's the one that's always gonna stick with me.

"See, I still think about her, Jimmy. I think about her every day. And I think about that thing that attacked her. It wasn't anything I'd ever heard of before or encountered since. I learned, though. I swear, I learned so much about that fucking thing, that one of a kind son of a bitch."

A new line, this one curving, hooking. It completed the first symbol. He started on the next.

"It took me a long time to be ready, to learn everything I needed to know. Well Jimmy, I'm ready now. I've got everything I need to destroy this fucking thing, and I intend to do just that, no doubt about it. Thing is, I need you to defeat it."

Jimmy stared up at him with horrified eyes. Realization blossomed there, catching like a brush fire.

"You son of a bitch! You're using me as bait?"

Charlie shrugged. "More or less, yeah."

"Why me?"

He chuckled. He hated to do it, but the dumb bastard's need to know amused him. "Because you wanted me here, you stupid prick! You invited me to come ride the storm out with you. How easy you want to make it for me? I need a flood; I need bait. Oh look! Here's a flood coming and a dumb piece of shit wants me to stay in his goddamn diner with him. Jesus, I couldn't make this shit up!"

Jimmy almost looked hurt. "That's it? That's your fucking reason? I ain't ever done shit to you, Charlie! And now you're doing this to me like it's some way of saying 'Thank you!'"

Charlie stopped carving, focused entirely on the man stretched out before him. "No, Jimmy. Think good and hard. Would I have done this to just anybody? No. It's never that easy. You don't want to hear the rest."

"Yes, I do."

"No you don't, Jimmy! I'm offering you a kindness, here. Just shut up and take it!"

"Fucking *tell* me!"

He shook his head. "Fine. I'm doing this because you're worthless."

Mills's eyes bugged wide, his jaw dropping open. Charlie saw shock, disbelief, and hurt all in the same expression.

"I mean it, Jimmy. You know what's going to happen in Sulfer. You've always known. We all do. This place is important. The folks who live here are important. One of these days we'll have to stand for the rest of the goddamn world, and we'll be the ones to hold back the fuckin' darkness. We're warriors, shit-splat. That's all we were ever meant to be. We use magic because one day we have to try our damndest to save the world with it.

"And what do you use it for? You keep your grill lit during a flood. You make your burgers taste slightly better than dogshit. You don't do a single thing worthwhile with it. You think it's a fucking parlor trick. You insult it.

"You don't deserve the magic in your veins, you little fuck. And ain't a soul in town that's gonna miss you once you're gone. That's why I'm using you."

"Charlie—"

"Shut up." A gesture locked the muscles in Mills's jaw, silencing him.

Charlie went back to work, carving deeper and deeper. Outside, the sun made its way toward the horizon.

"Tell me how much you love me, Charlie."

"More than a little. Almost as much as a fifty-dollar lapdance."

Night cloaked the attic in darkness so thick and hot it felt like desire. Charlie waited at the back of the room, leaning against a wall thick with dust and cobwebs. He didn't mind the mess. He had other things on his mind, gears turning slow and sure, concentrating one ticking instant at a time. Spells moved through his thoughts, strategies sticking and coming unglued. Despite all his research, he didn't know everything about the thing he was hunting.

He lit a cigarette and breathed deep. The cherry flared, illuminating the shadows closest to him. Nothing there, not that he expected anything. This far in, he sensed every living creature. Their energy called out to him, telling him everything he needed t.o know He blocked almost all the creatures—all the people— out, zeroing in one thing, one awful, terrible thing.

That thing was coming. It moved through the murky waters that filled Sulfer's streets with a hungry menace. It didn't quite swim, didn't quite scuttle. Its movements were a malevolent lurching that made as little sense as its very existence.

It entered Second Street, following something that called to it, something that was meat but also energy. Some long-dormant instinct warned against it, but hunger demanded inspection.

Charlie took another deep pull off his smoke. He looked to the open windows, listened to the gentle movements of the water beyond. Jimmy Mills lay unconscious ten feet in front of the glass. The blood loss had finally taken him maybe an hour earlier. His chest still rose and fell, but it was shallow, weak. He wouldn't last until morning, even if he didn't have a different fate in store. Poor bastard.

Crawford began to take another hit, but the splashing in the street stopped him. He felt a sudden fluttering in his stomach, and he knew the time had come. He removed the cigarette from his lips and held it at his side. His heart pounded behind his ribs, making his entire body vibrate. His hands shook with excitement and vengeance. He wanted to roar, but he didn't dare. He took a last, deep breath and held it.

Showtime.

It crossed the threshold a predator, confident but cautious. Charlie watched as the first hand reached through the window and grasped the floor. Its flesh was the color of spoiled milk, sagging just the slightest bit over powerful muscles. The talons on the end of its four webbed fingers were long as knifes, each hooked and catching the moonlight. The arm that followed was thick, strong. Another hand appeared, latching onto the wooden floor and pulling, the timber cracking and creaking under its strong grip. The creature pulled itself through, breaking the window frame as it forced its way into the attic.

The demon stood on all fours, its larger joints arching high above its body. It stood nearly eight feet tall. Silver light played off its shining, sickly hide. Muscles rippled under skin that was tight here, sagging there. Its head, a sleek, eyeless orb with a row of overlapping fangs, swiveled back and forth as if sizing up its new surroundings. Its jaw dropped open, and the demon screeched in a hollow way, wind through ruins.

Charlie fought the urge to want a weapon, fought the demanding need to charge and rip into the thing with his bare hands. If he did that now it would only mean a painful death. He had to do this, had to see it through to the goddamn end, and that meant he had to be patient.

He cataloged the things he knew about the creature: it was a water demon, a creature of hell that survived in the polluted waters of rivers, lakes, and oceans; its claws could infect you with the wasting disease that had killed Tammie; the disease had no cure; few had survived encounters with the beasts.

But few were Charlie Crawford, and few lived in a place like Sulfer, Indiana.

He watched as the monstrosity lumbered across the creaking boards. It found Jimmy and sniffed at his unmoving body. All but one of the sigils he'd carved into the man's chest glowed red in the demon's presence. The beacon had worked. Now he just had to hope the last carving—the one that now burned a cool blue—would perform its duties.

The demon opened its maw. Charlie felt a single stab of guilt before deciding Jimmy was lucky to be unconscious. In the next instant, the creature bit into Mills' bleeding chest, tearing flesh and cracking ribs. The cook's eyes snapped open, and there was an instant of agony and terror in them before they dimmed and closed once more.

Chewing sounds filled the night, wet smacking and dry crunching. The demon rumbled deep in its throat, a hungry sound, pleased.

Charlie's breath burned in his lungs, but he didn't dare release it. He had one chance to surprise the thing. He kept his eyes on Mills, saw the flesh at the edges of his wound liquefy and fall away. The wound expanded, its edge closing in on the blue sigil.

C'mon! he thought, willing the beast to take another bite. The mark would work either way, but—

His stomach flopped as he heard the demon swallow. It darted forward with surprising speed and took another bite.

And its teeth broke the sigil.

The sudden sound of electricity exploding through the creature's body pounded against Charlie's ears. The smell of ozone plunged down his nostrils despite his held breath. The beast jittered in place, sparks arcing off its body, dark smoke wafting into the still air. Flashes of light revealed the monster's horrible skeleton like x-rays.

The spell raced through Charlie's mind as he pushed away from the wall and charged across the floor. The demon slumped toward the floor before looking up, hearing the booted footfalls. Charlie was already in range, however, already raising the burning cigarette in front of his lips. He blew with everything he had, and his breath burst into flame as it crossed the glowing cherry.

The fireball struck the creature like a speeding eighteen-wheeler. Charlie felt the heat against his skin in the instant before the beast's scream ripped through his eardrums like razors. It reared up on its hind legs as the flames coursed over its flesh. A wet, fouling smell that reminded him of a garbage fire filled the air.

He smiled. "You remember me? Huh? You remember me, you horrible *fuck?*" He sucked in a breath, preparing to hit the demon with another burst of flame.

The monster's arm moved faster than Charlie could have imagined. It swung across the space to strike him with a backhand that felt like a wrecking ball. The floor disappeared as he sailed toward the back of the room. The mad thought *This is gonna hurt!* darted through his brain and then the pain arrived as he slammed into the brick wall.

The world threatened to go black on him. He shook his head, fighting the shadows that swirled at the edges of his vision. He heard thunder in the distance, coming closer. He realized it was the beast charging across the floor, coming for him. He dove to the side, moving blind. There was a crash as the demon collided with the rear wall.

Charlie searched for a spell. His brain felt scrambled, useless. Thoughts and ideas bounced around at lighting speed, beads of water on a hot skillet. He couldn't grab hold of any of them. The world around him slowed, and he stumbled through it punch drunk, wondering why his brain was a grease fire.

He heard a commotion behind him and turned to see what the hell was making such a racket. The demon was on its feet again, watching him with that eyeless face. Smoke and the remnants of flame rolled off its powerful body as it stretched, looking more like it had just crawled out of bed than slammed into a goddamn wall.

Charlie shook the last of the cobwebs free and backed up a step. His eyes never left the monster in front of him. What else could he use on this thing? How much more damage could it take and keep coming? Neither question turned up an answer. He blamed his rattled mind.

The demon stalked him, and he took another step backward. It was pushing him toward the window, toward the river. He knew it, and he didn't like it one bit. He wasn't going to beat this thing if it returned to the Ohio. He'd lose it, and he might not be able to lure it again. He'd fail.

He had to keep its attention.

"Does it hurt?" he said. "Looks like it hurts real fucking bad, you ugly bastard!" He took another step, and the floor nearly gave way beneath him. He glanced down and saw the splintered wood that remained from the demon's charge. He spoke a few words in a forgotten language, and the wood began to break apart even more, to crack like twigs beneath his weight.

He hit the demon with another spell, one he hadn't used since that night in the river nearly twenty years earlier. The building shuddered once when the shockwave struck, and the monster flew toward the back wall, hitting hard enough to bring bricks down on top of it. The windows shattered, raining glass into the river. A terrible creaking filled the attic, followed by a roar as the rearmost section of the roof caved in, collapsing on top of the demon.

Charlie laughed as rubble buried the monster. Dust and filth flew into his mouth, but he didn't care. He'd hurt the fucking thing, and that was enough to make him happy. He needed to kill it, though. He couldn't rest until he'd finished it off.

The beast wrestled loose of the timber and bricks, looking dazed and furious. It took a pair of shuffling steps, letting the broken stones fall off its back. It sniffed the air, searching.

"I'm right here," Charlie said. He stood perfectly still, afraid to shift his weight. The boards beneath his feet felt as though might collapse in the face of a spring breeze. He'd given Jimmy's place a pounding, all right. He just hoped it was in the condition he needed, weak enough for his trap to work but strong enough to remain standing.

The demon shook its head, let out a screech that shook the walls.

Charlie whispered a few words before smirking. "C'mon! Stop being such a pussy and *come get me!*"

The beast attacked. It leapt from its spot, jaw dropping open and terrible claws ready to shred flesh. Its roar filled the attic and escaped into the night.

Charlie jumped. His spell carried him impossibly high. His back slammed against the ceiling, and he began to fall again. He reached out and grabbed hold of the rafters, held on tight.

Below him, the demon slammed into the weakened floor. With a great crash, the floorboards gave way. The monster thrashed, searching for anything to stop its descent, but there was nothing. It fell through the floor and dropped into the dining room.

Charlie pushed off the rafters with everything he had, diving after the beast. For a single instant— screaming a spell at the top of his lungs—he felt like a superhero. Then he hit the demons with everything he had. The force of his impact was like a ton of steel dropping out of the sky. The demon screamed in pain, and Charlie felt its ribs shatter.

They hit the dining room floor and broke through, the world quaking around them. Charlie roared with fury as they entered the dark and slammed into the cobblestones that made up the floor of Jimmy Mills' basement. He heard a satisfying crumbling sound as the stones broke beneath them. Together, magician and demon fell into the building's original basement.

Together, they fell into the tomb.

He pounded his fists into the creature's flesh, fighting with every ounce of his anger. The demon shrieked beneath him, pain and hatred spilling into the dark. Red washed over Charlie's vision, taking hold. It burned through his being like a wildfire in July.

Something in the back of his brain screamed at him to get out of the darkness, but he ignored it. Nothing mattered but hurting this *thing,* making it pay for all of the pain it had caused.

He clawed at the demon's chest, anger and magic giving him the strength to tear through its flesh. Brackish water spilled over his hands, cold and awful. The sensation woke him from his rage. He remembered why he needed to get out, and in the same instant he heard the dry scuttling sounds all around him.

He looked up, finding the edge of the hole above him. He leapt, hoping he still had enough magic in his muscles to make the distance. He nearly fell short, but somehow managed to catch stones with his fingers. Biting back his scream, fighting the pain that surged through his arms, he clawed at the cobbles. He kicked with both legs and managed to gain a few inches. With a solid grip, he pulled himself from the hole, refusing to rest until he was clear of the abyss beneath him.

"Mother of hell!" he whispered as he rolled onto his back. From the tomb came the sounds of the demon's agonized screams and the tearing of its flesh. The soft clicking of bones accompanied the terrible sounds, and they made Charlie smile. Sulfer's dead had never liked being disturbed.

He'd won. It had taken so damn long and the cost had been high, but in the end it had been worth it. The thing that had killed Tammie was suffering, dying. Soon it would be gone, nothing but muddy water to mix with the bones of a past generation. One day something far worse would be coming down the pike, but right now that didn't matter. Tammie had been avenged, and that was good enough.

Charlie hugged himself and waited for the pain to go away. He began to laugh, and he laughed so long he began to cry.

"I'm sorry I couldn't save you."

And he was. Every goddamn day.

Charlie awoke in the darkness of the basement surprised to find he was still alive. His entire body sang with pain, and he could already tell which bones he'd broken during his tussle with the demon. His left collar bone and right tibia were the worst offenders. The two ribs would be okay, so long as they didn't puncture a lung. His left hand felt damn near shattered, but he never used it for much anyway. No big loss, really.

The nearby hole was silent. Maybe the dead had decided to continue their rest, or maybe they'd made up their minds to move on out of their resting place. Charlie almost laughed at the thought, picturing a few hundred waterlogged skeletons shagging ass out of their tomb only to find out they were in the middle of another flood. He started to chuckle, but his ribs told him how bad an idea that was.

He needed to get out of the basement. Maybe he was safe down here, and maybe he wasn't, but that didn't matter when all the food was one floor up. Maybe he could find enough supples to patch himself up, wait out the rest of the flood. It wasn't as though he had a whole lot of alternatives.

As carefully as he could, he crawled to the stairs. The journey was a slow, agonized one. He knew he might be able to save time by climbing to his good leg and hopping, but he didn't dare tempt the ribs, at least not right away. Once he reached the foot of the staircase, he grabbed hold of the wooden banister and pulled himself to his feet. Every motion brought new agony to his body, but his determination didn't falter.

The stairs looked impossibly tall. The climb might finish the job the demon had started. Charlie shook his head. In the end, it didn't matter. Something crazy in his brain that might have been determination had decided he would make it to the top of the stairs.

"C'mon, you boneheaded bastard," he said. "Start climbing."

And so he did.

The climb took an hour, but it was worth it.

He found her waiting on the other side of the glass storefront. She stood naked, still but for her dark hair, which danced through the currents like smoke.

Charlie took a deep breath, blinked. It was really her. He'd seen the face in his dreams thousands of times. Her smile had lit his night like a candle, and her body had sliced through endless waters. So many years later, she still looked the same, as eternal as the Ohio herself.

"Tammie." The name echoed through the ruins of Jimmy Mills' diner, rippling like sorrowful currents.

Her expression did not change. She pressed her hands to the glass, and her eyes locked on his.

He approached slowly, cautiously. If his broken bones gave him pain, he didn't feel it. His mind only registered Tammie. He wanted to believe it was a miracle, but he knew it was probably something worse. Miracles didn't take place in Sulfer.

But she was here. She was right in front of him, hands to the glass.

He reached the doorway and stood across from her. His palm found the glass and pressed. He felt the cool of the river, but there was a strange warmth there, something he hadn't felt since he'd lost this woman so many years before.

He looked into her eyes. They returned his gaze. They were kind, happy.

"I miss you," he said.

She nodded, and he felt his palms grow warmer.

"There hasn't been anybody else. I couldn't. I don't know if you wanted that, but it doesn't matter. I couldn't even imagine somebody other than you."

She gave no noticeable reaction. He didn't know what that might mean. Instead of trying to sort it out, he let his forehead rest against the glass. Memories flowed through his mind like silt, settling, polluting. There were some beautiful things in there, but almost everything after Tammie's death had been ugly.

"I would have followed, but you said I'm important. Maybe I am. I don't feel like it—just feel like a bastard—but maybe you were right. So I'll stick around until I'm done, then I'll come for you."

He looked at her. She smiled. Her head tilted into a nod. She shifted forward, and suddenly her lips found the glass.

Charlie closed his eyes and returned her kiss.

She was gone when he looked again. He knew she

would be. It was okay, though. He knew where she was now, knew for sure. When he was finally done—when it was all finished—he would find her. Her smile would light the way.

SAFE HOUSE

August 14th

We attacked the State Police headquarters in Mason today, and just like that, we're rolling. It's been a long time coming (and I'll admit it, there were times I thought we'd never make it this far), but now the day is finally here. We're changing the world. Or at least saving this country.

Quickly, I want to praise Jonathan Simms, the first martyr of our cause. He understood how important it was that this action not lead back to us, that the movement is more important than the survival of its players. That's why the third and final of the pressure cooker bombs he set off was in the passenger seat of his patrol car while he sat behind the wheel. This particular thread ends with him. While he will not receive the recognition he deserves, he will have our gratitude from now until the end. Thank you, Jonathan. Despite your job with the State, you proved yourself a good man.

I told Jenny I'm leaving her and the kids, that I've been fucking another woman and that I'm sick of looking at them day in and day out. Far as she knows,

I'm running off to Vegas to live with a woman I refused to name. Told her it didn't matter, that the only part I cared about was being free of her and her bullshit. She cried a lot, and it hurt like hell.

"How can you do this with everything happening out there?" Her voice was thick with tears and confusion. "Goddammit, Brad! We're your family. You're supposed to take care of your family."

"I want out of this family," I said. Did a pretty good job of acting like I meant it, too. "I'm sick to death of this family. Keep my last check. Consider it a parting gift."

We were in the kitchen when I told her, the kids at school, and she ripped open the cabinet and started hurling plates at me. One after another, she sent them flying toward me. I dodged most of them, let them shatter against the wall and rain shards of ceramic to the floor, but I let a couple hit me. All things considered, I felt I deserved it. They couldn't come with me, and there was no way to explain to them where I was going without putting everything at risk. Once we're done, I can come back for them. I can take care of them. Right now, it's just too risky. The others are making similar sacrifices.

Yeah, a lot of that depends on if we survive and if we make it back. That's the whole reason we're heading to the safe house, though.

"You asshole," Jenny said. She screamed at me from the kitchen floor, where she'd curled up like a dead spider. "I hope the two of you are real goddamn happy."

Standing over her, I wanted to say I was sorry. Instead, I left.

August 15th

We met at the safe house, a log cabin deep in the Kentucky hills. Kind of a cliché, and I'm not exactly happy about it. A log cabin? Makes it look like we're a bunch of militia rednecks. We're not. Still, it belonged to somebody deep in the organization, so deep I've never met them. Hopefully, that means they're so deep the feds won't track us down. Organization is key to making it through this.

There are six of us. Well, there were supposed to be. Mitchell, a schoolteacher from Frankfort, brought his wife, so there are seven. He tried to explain, but the rest of us didn't feel like listening. The man screwed up, breached damn near every protocol we established. Ratner said we should boot her, maybe send both of them packing, but the idea didn't gain much traction. For now, there are seven of us. Either Mitchell's wife (her name's Renee) will come around or she won't. We'll keep an eye on her and figure things out.

It's pretty hard to gauge everybody's moods. Maybe it's because I'm still thinking about Jenny and the kids.

Telling myself they'll understand when I return doesn't exactly help. Way back in the deeper corners of my brain, I don't think they will understand. No matter when I show up, no matter how many times I tell them it's for the greater good, I'll still be the man who abandoned them when the entire country was under attack and heading straight to hell. I'll be the asshole Jenny said I was, and I won't be able to deny it.

Ratner seems more pissed than anything. Mitchell and Renee have him on edge, but he needs to get past that. I've known Ratner for years. Hell, we were Sunday football buddies before he recruited me to the cause. He showed up at the cabin with all his hair chopped off and bags under his eyes. Those eyes have been burning since. Mitchell only made things worse, I guess.

Sidney, a nurse from Lexington, just stays quiet and sits near the window. She hasn't said much, and I wonder who or what she left behind. We need somebody with medical expertise, though. She fits the bill, and it's not like anyone forced her to join the cause.

Davey and Joe are brothers. Davey served in the marines, and Joe's supposed to be some amazing mechanic. He was regular army. They spent most of the day going through our available vehicles, weapons, and other supplies. It's good to have some people here with real experience. I can't imagine how helpful that will be.

So now we wait for our orders. Any day now, we should know our next move. I hope it's a big one. Maybe that will take my mind off Jenny and the boys.

August 17th

There was an argument today. Ratner's been shooting Mitchell and Renee dirty looks like you wouldn't believe, refusing to talk to anyone other than to mutter a few words about discipline and protocol and the way things are supposed to work. More than a few times, I've caught him giving the pair of them the stink eye from across the cabin. I understand, because Mitchell's spending a lot more time trying to bring Renee around than worrying about our goals, but Ratner's brooding isn't helping.

Not that he's brooding anymore. After today's blowup, it's all pretty much out in the open.

She asked if we had anything we could cook. Big mistake. We've got a basement stocked with MREs and canned goods, but so far we haven't turned up much through hunting. I guess Mitchell didn't explain the situation to her. Or maybe he did and she just didn't get it.

"Really? You guys don't even have some eggs or ham?"

Ratner had been sitting on the ratty couch that fills the center of the living room. With a single kick, he sent an old coffee table skidding halfway to the fireplace. "Does Paris Hilton want a mimosa and a massage, too?" he asked. His voice was acidic.

Renee held up both hands, surrendering. "Sorry, okay? I didn't mean it."

"Oh, you meant it." Ratner jumped off the couch and stomped toward the kitchen. I tried to block him, but he pushed me aside. "Did Mitchell tell you this was a vacation? That this is a goddamn spa? You pampered stack of garbage."

That got Mitchell's attention. "Watch yourself, there."

"Me? Please! You should know better, Mitchell. You think she could survive when we're bottomed out? She's the exact kind of spoon-fed pissant we're trying to get rid of!"

"Get rid of?" Renee asked. Her tone told us Mitchell hadn't exactly filled her in on every detail. Of course, it wasn't like I'd found a way to explain to Jenny that we were dragging the country back to zero, creating a place where the bureaucracy is dead and only those fit to survive will do so.

By this point, we'd all gathered in the kitchen. I looked at Davey and Joe. They appeared ready to pull Ratner and Mitchell apart or drop them to the floor, whichever needed doing. However, Ratner stormed out of the cabin rather than keep pushing. Joe followed him out, and Davey ushered Mitchell and Renee down to the basement, where I hoped he explained some things to her. Sidney and I just shared a shrug. At least things hadn't been worse.

No orders yet. To a degree, we're flying blind. Part of keeping the safe house under the radar is not using too much power, keeping the heat down. That means we don't get a lot of news outside of brief checks on the internet and radio. Maybe that sounds paranoid, but I just think it's smart.

August 18th

Joe tore us from sleep just after two in the morning. Part of me wants to say something less dramatic, like he woke us, but that's not what he did. My eyes popped open when a hand clamped over my mouth. I saw Joe standing over me, a finger to his lips. Once I gave him a tiny nod, he let go of my mouth and I sat up. That's when I saw Ratner and Sidney in my doorway. All of them were armed, and Joe slipped a Glock into my hand before I could ask him what was going on.

"Somebody outside," Joe said. He spoke in a flat whisper, and his eyes ticked toward the window.

I'll admit, those two words filled me with a sense of relief. When I hadn't seen Mitchell and his wife with the rest, I'd thought the others had decided it was time to do something about them. Why I'd dread such an action, I don't know. More than anything, I believe in the cause. If they had to die in order to serve that cause, fine...

I climbed out of bed and slipped my feet into a pair of tennis shoes. Quietly, I joined the others in the hallway. Davey led Mitchell and his wife out of their room. Renee looked terrified, so maybe she finally understood the measure of things.

"Something moving through the woods to the east," Joe said. "Trying to be quiet, but I heard footsteps loud and clear."

"Could be a deer," Sidney said.

"Doesn't matter. We're supposed to be cautious."

"So we check it out," Ratner said. "Everybody stays alert."

Renee shook her head, blond hair whipping in the darkness. "I don't want to go out there."

"We don't want you out there, Paris."

"Stop calling me that."

Mitchell pulled her close. "I can stay back with her, keep an eye on things."

Ratner took a turn shaking his head. "No deal. I don't trust the two of you alone."

"You can trust her," Mitchell said.

"Sid, you want to hang back with her?" Davey asked.

I watched annoyance and disappointment wage a silent war in Sidney's eyes. "Fine," she said. "Anything gets past you, I'll handle it."

"That's what I like to hear." Then, Davey led Ratner out the cabin's back door, and I followed Joe out the front.

The night was clear and calm, a little cooler than I'd expected. Goosebumps erupted along my arms and legs, and I gripped the pistol with both hands, hoping the action might quell the shivers racing through me. I won't pretend nerves didn't play at least a small part. With each step, I half-expected to be lit up from above, a black helicopter nailing me to the ground with a spotlight. From there I'd either be shoved to the forest floor by federal agents of just have my switch flipped by bullets.

Heading toward the forest's edge, I shook off the heavy thoughts. They were nothing more than distractions, a good way to get killed. If Joe really had heard something, any threats would be on the ground. I pressed my back to a tree as Joe did the same ten yards from me. Holding my breath, I listened to the night. It didn't answer. A heavy silence blanketed the forest, and I couldn't even hear Davey and Ratner on the other side of the cabin.

I turned and gave Joe a look. He held a finger to his lips and pointed deeper into the trees. Maybe he heard something I didn't. A second later, a single rustling footstep caught my attention. The snap of a twig followed it. Joe eased into a crouch, the shotgun hard against his shoulder, and I did the same. He pushed away from the tree and started into the forest. Whoever was out there was close, no more than twenty yards, concealed by darkness and trees and the thick vegetation that all but choked the forest floor. As I followed Joe, I wondered what we might find, what we'd have to do. Were we seconds from a firefight? We hadn't thought to put on our vests. Stupid.

We closed to within ten feet of the snapping twig, and then a tortured screech stopped us. The agonized sound peeled out of the brush. I jumped, nearly firing a shot into the ground, and I saw Joe curl in a tighter posture. He threw a look over his shoulder and waved for me to follow, and then he was out of his crouch and charging forward, rushing toward what sounded like an animal being tortured. I broke right as he went left, determined to surround whatever was close and dangerous, but the underbrush slowed me. Even sprinting, I had to wrestle my way through bushes and branches and knotty vines. The screams died off before I joined Joe. By then, we heard Davey and Ratner rushing toward us.

When Joe lowered his weapon, I did the same. Something had been there, but it was gone now. Joe held up a hand as the others approached, and their rushing footsteps became slow and cautious, just shy of casual. He pointed toward the ground, and the rest of us looked. Davey stooped beside the mess and played a penlight over it.

If I had to guess, I'd say it used to be a rabbit. I saw a lot of fur and a lot of blood spread across the ground, but little I'd call identifiable. Something had torn the little bastard apart, hadn't killed it or tortured it so much as ruined it.

"Coyote?" Ratner asked.

Joe shrugged. "Maybe a bobcat."

Davey prodded a scrap of fur with the muzzle of his weapon. "Would have been nice if it had left some meat behind."

"Let's do a quick sweep and head back in."

We agreed and got to work. Five minutes later, we decided we were indeed alone, and we went back to bed. Moving forward, I just have to remember to keep my eyes open in the woods. Don't want to wind up face to face with a bobcat.

August 20ᵗʰ

Renee's gone. Mitchell swears he doesn't know where she went, that he woke to find her gone, no note left behind and the few belongings she'd brought right where he'd last seen them. Just in case, we have him cuffed to a chair. Honestly, I don't think it's some grand plan of theirs. Most likely, she got scared and ran in the middle of the night, left everything behind and didn't bother taking one of the vehicles because she didn't want to wake anyone.

At the heart of it all, her being gone really makes things rough for us. The only scenario we can think of that doesn't end with her giving away our position involves her being found by either us or whatever tore apart that animal. Right now, the others are out searching the forest. It's my turn to keep an eye on Mitchell. We figure if he wasn't in on it, there's still an outside chance his wife will come back for him. Yeah, that idea hinges on Renee being an idiot, but there's no end to the idiots out there.

Tried talking to Mitchell a bit. Didn't go well.

"Did she talk about leaving?"

"No. I mean, she didn't want to come here. The first night, she wanted to go, said we were paranoid. I explained it to her, though. Maybe she hadn't come around completely, but she was getting there."

"You explained it to her?" I couldn't believe he was serious.

"I know my wife. She loves me, okay? We communicate. I didn't have to abandon her to prove it, either."

"Watch it, Mitchell."

"Please." He got this look on his face like he'd just tasted something rotten. "I'm not an idiot. If they don't find her out there, I'm the one who's gonna get tortured for it. Somebody's going to think I know something."

I shook my head, hoping he wouldn't realize I'd already considered the idea. "You want coffee?" I asked. Seemed like a good way to veer off that road.

"I'm fine." He didn't look happy.

"Well, I can use some coffee. Everybody else will need some, too. Probably got a long day ahead of all of us."

"Guess it might get real long." I guess he was still thinking about torture. Who could blame him?

As I bustled around the cabin's kitchen, getting a pot ready to brew, I didn't talk to Mitchell. Didn't even look at him. Every time I saw him, I felt my anger grow a little hotter, like an ember in a gentle breeze, threatening to catch. A quick glance out the window didn't show anybody marching back, Renee in tow.

"What was I supposed to do?" Mitchell asked. "She's my wife. That's…it's like she's a part of me. I'm really just supposed to leave that behind?"

That breeze picked up a little, and the ember glowed. I saw Jenny's face as I told her there was someone else and that I was leaving. Tears spilled down her face. Her lips trembled and pulled back to show grinding teeth. Somewhere in the house, the kids wailed.

I waited for the coffee, staring at a block of knives on the kitchen counter. My knuckles burned, and I stuffed my fists into my pockets.

The back door opened and Sidney entered. She looked tired, her face coated in a thin sheen of sweat and dirt.

"Anything?" I asked.

"Joe thinks he might have found some tracks. Maybe. Anything from Mitchell?"

"He thinks he's the only one who loves his family." Petty, but it felt good.

"I never said that."

I poured Sidney a cup of coffee, and she sipped at it while she stared down Mitchell. Part of me expected her to throw it in his face, but she didn't.

"Did you help her go?" she asked.

"What?"

"You heard me, Mitchell. Answer the question. If you answer it, it'll be okay. We just need to protect the mission. No one will get hurt."

He shook his head and looked at his feet. "I woke up, and she was gone. That's all."

"Where would she go?"

He shrugged without looking up. "Back to the house, maybe? Her mother's? If she didn't take a car, I don't really know. I love the woman, but she's not a hiker. Doesn't even like camping. The idea that she just took off...."

"It's a little hard to swallow," I said. Silence filled the air between us. I decided to down a cup of brew and take Sidney's place in the forest.

"They went east, Joe and Ratner," she said as I opened the back door. "Davey's headed west or northwest. Pick a direction and go. Keep your eyes open."

"Will do."

I really thought I'd just go out and look for her, but I found some things that really bugged me. Maybe I should go ahead and get into it, but I'm tired and Ratner keeps shouting. Mitchell's still crying, and I can't concentrate. I'll get it down tomorrow.

Good night.

August 21ˢᵗ

I need to explain what I found in the forest, but I also need to talk about last night and what happened between Ratner and Mitchell. The rest of us are partly responsible, I guess. We let it happen. There's just this anxiety and a good chunk of paranoia. What if Renee tells the authorities? Do we need to bug out? A fair amount of variables, and variables create stress.

"Where did she go? Where did she go, *Mitchell?*" Ratner kept saying it over and over again, getting louder each time. He stalked in circles around the chair where Mitchell sat, leering in for emphasis now and then. Something in his eyes burned. More than anger, it was a bright and broken thing, like his brain had cracked and caught fire.

For his part, Mitchell did his best to not look scared. His act wasn't very convincing. "I already told—"

"Where did she go?"

"I don't—"

"Where did she *go*, Mitchell?"

Davey stood at the back door, watching with narrowed eyes. Sidney stayed in the kitchen, pretending she was working on something. I'd watched her get steadily more agitated as Ratner worked his mantra, though. I think he was getting to her more than Mitchell. During any instant of silence, I listened for Joe's footsteps outside. I trusted him, but what I'd found in the woods had me spooked.

"Where did she go?"

"Dude, sit down and breathe," Davey said. His voice sounded tired. "Even if he knows, he isn't going to tell. Just sit down and relax. We'll sort our next move here in a bit."

"*Where did she go, Mitchell?*"

Ratner dove on the guy before any of us could realize he was moving. Both men crashed to the floor, cracking the wooden chair beneath their weight, and Ratner took hold of Mitchell's throat. He stopped using words and just screamed in short, mad bleats. With each exclamation, he shook Mitchell by the neck. I ran to stop him, and I heard Mitchell's head bounce off the floor before I could reach them.

As I climbed onto Ratner's back and tried to wrestle him loose, I heard a harsh sound that was almost a cluck from Mitchell. He wasn't getting so much as a gasp of air. Ratner kept shaking him, and his body felt hard as stone as I wrapped my arms around him. Mitchell's skull bounced off the floor again. I watched his eyes roll back in his head and his body go limp, and that just made Ratner throttle him harder.

Davey's arms joined mine, and together we finally ripped Ratner free of the comatose body he was strangling. With each of us wrestling an arm, we dragged him toward the kitchen. He kept screaming, violent bursts of random sound filling the cabin. I lost control of his left arm, and he threw a fist over his right shoulder, barely missing Davey's temple. As Sidney rushed past us to check on Mitchell, I fought to grab hold of Ratner's arm again. Trying to control a fire hose was probably easier.

Sidney crouched beside Mitchell, taking his face in her hands, and we rushed Ratner out the back door. I'd known the man for years, considered him one of my better friends, but I'd never seen his temper explode like this.

"Easy," Davey said.

Joe ran around the cabin's corner, rifle butt hard against his shoulder, and stopped short when he saw us. "What in hell...?"

"Easy, dude. C'mon. Ratner, listen to my voice and chill out."

It took time, but Ratner's breathing did ease from shouts and screams and gulps to labored huffs and then finally slow, even breaths.

"You okay?" I asked.

He nodded. "I'm fine. Just...just a lot of shit in my head right now."

"We all got that. Gotta keep cool, right?"

"He never should have brought his wife."

"I know. He fucked up. All we can—"

"He never should have brought his wife." This time, he didn't wait around for me to say something. With a disgusted shake of his head, he pushed through us and walked into the woods. I started after him, but Davey gave my shoulder a squeeze and stopped me.

"Just give him some time."

I nodded, but Davey hadn't seen what I'd seen out there. He didn't know.

Guess I can talk about what was in the woods now. Ratner came back after twenty minutes, and Sidney said Mitchell's got a minor concussion and should be okay. Hell, Ratner even apologized. Nothing's really solved, since Renee's still missing and we don't know our next move, but the lid's been put back in place. I guess that counts for something. Maybe not progress, but a holding pattern.

So, the woods. When I left the cabin, I headed south, which took me deeper into the valley. I had my eyes peeled and my pistol in hand. Not sure if I was afraid of stumbling across police or agents or what. Maybe I thought I could solve the Renee situation if I came across her. I don't like admitting it, but she was a liability, and a single bullet to the back of her head would solve a lot of problems. Yeah, that's a real mercenary way of looking at it, but both sides take casualties in a war. Sooner or later, that's a fact you just have to accept.

The deeper I trudged into the valley, the darker everything became. Full trees choked out most of the sunlight, and the slopes of the hills surrounding me took care of almost all the rest. Soon, the air around me was humid but cool, almost cold. Several times, I nearly tumbled down the hill's steep grade, only a last second grab at a tree stopping me. If Renee had been anywhere nearby, she would have heard me.

By the time I reached the valley floor, I was almost out of breath. My pulse beat in my skull, and I tucked the pistol into my waistband so I could rub both temples while I leaned against the nearest trunk. Looking up the hill, I couldn't think of anything but how much that walk back was going to suck.

Once my breathing and heart rate slowed to their normal pace, I examined the valley, looking for some sign Renee had passed. There were no footprints in the old foliage or snapped branches, no trace of Renee. Or there were and I couldn't find them. I saw trees and a cover of leaves in various stages of rot, some thick tangles of underbrush. That's it. Searching for clues only pointed out that I was no tracker.

With nothing else to do, I picked a direction (left) and started moving. My shirt was cold and damp against my back, and that kept my nerves twitching. I tried to move as quietly as possible, but my footsteps were the only thing I could hear. The shifting of old leaves filled my head, a whisper that dug deeper and deeper.

I'm not sure how long I traveled down the valley before I saw the shack. It didn't feel like that long, but it's hard to tell without the sun. And it was twilight before I reached the cabin again.

A part of me wanted to call the crumbling wooden structure I found a cabin, but it was barely as large as a backyard storage shed. It stood about fifty feet up the opposite hillside on a tiny patch of even ground. Boards that had faded to an ash gray clung to each other desperately. There was no door or windows, just an opening lined with splinters like teeth.

I ducked behind a tree and peered around the trunk, examining the shack from a distance. If Renee had made a break for it, would she see that wooden structure and hole up? Maybe she would, but maybe she'd just set some kind of trap and keep going. The thought almost made me chuckle. Like Renee had shown she could set even the most simple of traps. As far as I can tell, she lacks even the most basic of survival skills, and the way she balked at Mitchell's sudden reveal told me he hadn't bothered teaching her any.

Counting to thirty, I continued watching the shed. When I reached my magic number with no sign of Renee or anyone else, I stepped out from behind the tree and approached. I kept my weapon ready. The slightest sign of movement, and I would put it down. Maybe I didn't realize it at the time, but I do now. My nerves were stretched thin as fishing line. We'd done a good and thorough job of scouting the locations of our safe houses. How had anyone missed something like a shack? It was a careless thing, and it made me wonder what else had been missed.

A heavy stillness surrounded me as I crept closer to the shack, like the forest was holding its breath. Even my footsteps were silent, and I'm not exactly an expert when it comes to stealth. Maybe it was my senses playing tricks on me or my thoughts being too loud. Something like that.

I reached the shack without seeing so much as a hint that anyone was inside. With my back plastered to the outside wall, I threw a quick glance inside. After a second look, I decided the place was deserted and entered.

Really, I don't know what I was expecting. The place was tiny. To the left of the doorway, a thin mattress that had probably been ripped off a cot filled the dirt floor. A small dresser sporting three drawers stood across from the entrance, and I tried to imagine someone wrestling actual furniture into the valley. It maybe should have given me a chuckle, but instead it just left me confused. Leaves had blown in, dusting both the mattress and the ground. The shack looked like it had been abandoned for some time, months at the very least. A thick layer of dust coated the dresser, and the leaves had clogged the space beneath it.

Releasing a breath I hadn't realized I was holding, I stepped through the doorway and approached the dresser. The air inside the shack was colder, and the absence of sunlight was almost total. I reached the piece of furniture before my eyes adjusted, and I had to spend a few moments waiting for them to catch up.

When I could finally see again, I placed my gun on top of the dresser and opened the top drawer. It slid out in a series of catches and squealing jerks, requiring more effort that I'd expected. Save a few more of the leaves, it was empty. Giving it some of my shoulder, I shoved the drawer back home.

The second drawer opened a little easier, the old, dry wood not screaming nearly as much. Again, nothing but a few leaves and a quick swirl of dust that pirouetted into the air. I sneezed, wiped my nose on my sleeve, and then wrestled the drawer shut.

As I eyed the bottom drawer, I listened for footsteps or breathing, any sign I might not be alone. I heard nothing. A quick look over my shoulder convinced me

Renee wasn't sneaking up on me with a rock in her hand.

I pulled on the bottom drawer, and it only opened an inch or two before it stuck. Another tug didn't do much to help. I wiggled it back and forth, and it slid a fraction of an inch. A musty, almost spicy scent drifted from the drawer, and I guessed there was something more than dust and leaves inside. Bracing my shoulder against the dresser, I pushed the furniture against the wall and yanked at the drawer. It jerked open a few more inches, and then my next violent pull freed the wood almost completely. The drawer open, I peered inside, and then I clamped a hand over my mouth before I could scream.

At first glance, I thought someone had nailed an old steak or piece of roast inside the bottom drawer. Within seconds, however, I recognized the muscle as a heart. The brown and gray piece of meat barely held onto its shape, but the size told me it just might be human. It didn't smell bad, like I'd expect a rotting heart to, but just gave off that spicy scent. A dull gray nail held it in place. Several small, white objects surrounded it, and it took me a moment to realize I was looking at a scattering of teeth and finger bones.

Something slammed against the shack's rear wall hard enough to make the dresser jump. I screamed, hand over mouth or not, and leaped toward the doorway. Whatever was outside struck the back of the structure again, and I heard wood splinter. I remembered my pistol. Snatching the weapon from the dresser, I thumbed off the safety as quickly as my shaking hands would let me.

A third impact rocked the shack, and then a desperate scrabbling sound filled the air. It reminded me of a dog trying to paw its way in the back door. A large dog. I looked down at the 9mm in my hands and wondered if I could put down a coyote with it. Then, I wondered if there might be bears in the area. I should know better. Knowing how to survive is all a part of our grand plan, but fear knocked all that knowledge out of me.

Easing toward the doorway, I took several deep breaths. With each, I felt my nerves calm just a little. When I lifted the handgun toward the back wall and saw my hands weren't shaking, I decided it was time.

I rushed out the doorway, the 9mm still up in front of me. My footsteps sounded way too loud in the old leaves, so whatever was trying to bust into the shack had to hear me. Refusing to run just so it could rake claws down my back, I ran to the right, taking a wide arc around the shack. A dozens steps took me from the doorway to the back wall.

Nothing. I circled the shack three times, convinced with each corner I rounded that I'd come face to face with the world's stealthiest grizzly, but I never saw a thing. I couldn't even find a trace of an animal. The rear wall had been clawed to hell and back, though. Deep wounds in the wood like somebody had torn at it with long, wicked knives. Looking at the wall made me remember the frantic scrabbling I'd heard, and a violent shiver traveled through me. I couldn't handle any more, so I raced away from the shack and started the climb back to the cabin. Renee or no Renee, I was done with the valley.

I know I need to tell the others. What I found at the shack, what happened there…I can't just keep that to myself. The thing is, it's so weird. I tell everybody about it, and their two options are freaking out or not believing me. When you add in Renee's disappearance, Ratner's anger, and Mitchell being cuffed in the living room…well, I just don't know if bringing up the shack is the best idea.

I have to tell them, though. Right?

August 22nd

Jesus Christ! I'm sitting here, struggling to keep my hands from shaking so bad my writing isn't legible. If things were bad before, now they've taken a turn into god-fucking-awful.

Joe's dead. I guess that's the first thing to get out in the open. It's a terrible loss, because he was one of our most dependable people. Real military training, which now only Davey can say he has. Ratner and I aren't bad at what we do (we wouldn't have been welcomed if we were), but we're at least a step behind Davey and Joe. Just a step behind Davey now, I guess. Shit, this is all going down the tubes.

What happened was a scream woke me up. It woke all of us. Just this long, high-pitched shriek that didn't feel like it was going to end.

I jumped out of bed and grabbed the 9mm before I was even aware of my surroundings. That scream had me instantly wired, and I remembered the impacts and the scratches at the shack, the heart and teeth and bones in the drawer. In that moment, I bit back a scream of my own and turned toward the door. Davey rushed past, a shotgun in his hands, and Ratner followed. By the time I reached the hallway, I heard a man's screams join them. I thought it was Mitchell, but I couldn't be sure.

My senses were almost overloaded when I entered the living room. Both screams buzzed in my ears like they came from a bad speaker. When Davey clicked on the light, it was too bright, its harsh, white glare singeing my eyes.

The scream came from Renee. I sure as hell wasn't expecting that. She stood in the center of the living room, naked save her bra and panties and a day's worth of mud and leaves. Fresh blood caked her hands, had been smeared halfway to her elbows. Her eyes were wide open and staring at nothing. Behind her, Mitchell screamed from the chair where he was still cuffed. When he finally formed a word, it was his wife's name over and over again.

Renee stopped screaming long enough to suck in a breath. She launched right back into the same note. A shrieking statue, she didn't move an inch. Her expression didn't change. The seconds ticked by, and she didn't do a goddamn thing but scream, Mitchell shouting her name like a backup singer.

Sidney stepped past us, a single hand raised. "Renee? Renee, it's Sidney. Do you remember me?" If Renee heard her, she didn't show it.

As Sidney took another step forward, it occurred to me that Joe should have been on watch. He wasn't in the living room though, and Renee had made it past him. For some reason, I didn't make the connection between his absence and the blood on her hands. That buzzing scream must have been screwing with my brain.

"Renee, I need you to calm down, okay? Can you do that? Can you calm down?"

Mitchell joined in, only his voice was frantic and raw. "Renee, baby, you need to stop. What's wrong? Tell me what's wrong. You need to fucking stop!"

"Everybody *shut up!*" Ratner's voice boomed over everything else. It sounded too much like those bleating cries he'd made as he slammed Mitchell's skull into the floor. He took a pair of steps toward Renee, only he kept his handgun in front of him, the barrel aimed at her face.

Mitchell jumped in his chair, sending it crashing to the floor. "You motherfucker! Don't you point that fucking thing at her!"

"Somebody shut her up before I plug her."

"Don't you do it!"

"Somebody shut her up!"

Mitchell roared, a sound of pure rage and desperation, and Ratner shifted his aim. The gunshot deafened us all, and the back of Mitchell's head disappeared in a fan of red and gray muck.

I staggered back a step, lifting my shoulder to one ear as though it might stop the terrible pain and buzzing that filled my entire skull. Ratner lowered his handgun to his side and just stared at the blood pooling beneath the man he'd killed.

It took me a second to remember Renee. When I finally looked at her, I could only guess if she was still screaming or not. Her face remained frozen in place, so I guess she was. Sidney had collapsed to her knees in front of her, hands pressed to her ears. Renee didn't appear to notice.

The pain in my head was too great to let me react when Renee moved. With a strange calm, she lifted her hands to her face. I wasn't even sure anyone else had noticed. Could be their ears took all their attention. Or Mitchell's body. Either way, no one moved to stop her, not even me. I didn't do a damn thing but watch as she worked her fingers into her open mouth, stretched her lips wide, and then ripped open her cheeks. I saw the skin stretch and then tear, saw blood pour from the ragged wounds she created with her hands, and I didn't do a goddamn thing to stop her. Maybe I should have tackled her or pleaded with her, done anything other than watch.

Look, I know I could have done more. I'm not delusional, and I'm not trying to pretend I'm something I'm not. When she tore into her face with her hands, I should have done something. In a way, it was like watching a car crash. Everything just drifted into slow motion.

Sidney reacted first, moving Renee to the couch and shoving her down. Frantically, she tried to grab hold of the woman's fists and keep her from hurting herself, but Renee ignored her, fingers working on her face like claws. Only when Davey came up behind her and took hold of both arms did she stop.

Then, it was like someone had flipped a switch. Renee stopped attacking herself and let her hands drop to her sides. She stared straight ahead. Blood kept pouring from her ruined cheeks, and Sidney ran to get bandages.

All of that happened hours ago. Now, we've got Renee tied down in her bed, the bottom half of her face covered in bandages that might already be soaked through. Since we're short on supplies, Davey took some leather belts and nailed them to the wall, used those to secure her wrists and ankles. I had to help Ratner bury Mitchell's body. The entire time, he just kept saying, "He wasn't an alpha," like that excused him murdering one of our own. A part of me thinks Ratner would have done it sooner or later. He's... slipping. I think the stress is getting to him, but I can't be sure. I tried talking to Davey about it, but he was busy burying Joe.

That's right, Joe's dead. We found him at the edge of the forest, his eyes gouged out and his throat ripped open. That explains the blood on Renee's hands, at least. It doesn't explain Renee at all, though. Where did she go? Why did she come back? Why did she do those things, and then why did she just stop? She hasn't made a peep since Davey got her hands away from her face, hasn't looked any direction except forward. It's like something burnt out in her mind.

I need to tell them about the shack. And maybe we need to get the hell out of here.

August 23rd

Today, I showed Ratner and Davey the shack. Sidney wanted to see it, but she had to stay behind and watch after Renee. Before sitting around the breakfast table and trudging down into the valley, Ratner asked why I hadn't told them sooner. Every time he asked, I couldn't do anything but shrug.

"Ease off," Davey said when Ratner asked once again as we reached the valley's bottom.

"Ease off?" Ratner asked. "Hey, I'm just doing my part. That's what we're all supposed to be doing, right? So why isn't he doing his?"

I let the remark slide off my back. Arguing with Ratner wasn't going to improve matters.

"Where's the place?" Davey asked.

Pointing, I led the way. Within a few minutes, I spotted the shack jutting from the hillside like a tumor. "That's it."

Ratner scoffed. "That? It's a piece of shit."

"I said it was a shack. What were you expecting?"

He shook his head and gave us a dismissive chuckle, then started tromping up the hill. We followed. I looked to Davey for some kind of support, but he was taking in the forest, eyes never hovering over any one spot for longer than a second. At least one of us was still alert. A night with so little sleep had left me exhausted. Everything felt a little softer than it should be, edges blurring all around me. Not good.

"Ratner, weapon ready," Davey said. Ratner waved a hand and then drew his handgun and prepped it.

We were still maybe twenty yards back when Ratner reached the doorway and peered inside. He froze, standing in the doorway as we approached. When we stepped behind him, the tension drained from his posture, and he laughed.

"That's some scary stuff," he said. "I can see why we're crapping our pants."

I almost said something, but then I looked past Ratner and into the shack. The dresser and mattress were both gone. In their place, the bare branches of a thorn bush filled the space, choking the interior so thoroughly there was no room to step inside. The tangle of branches was old, the dried-out gray of a plant that was just shy of dead. I couldn't pretend this was new growth, even if I could convince myself such a bush might grow in two days.

Without a word, I left the doorway and rushed around the shack. I reached the rear wall and kicked up leaves as I stumbled to a halt. Nothing. Not so much as a single scratch marred the lumber. The boards were old and dry and cracking, but nothing had attacked them.

"Son of a bitch." I whispered the words to no one, but Davey and Ratner still heard me.

"What is it?" Davey asked.

I had no explanation to give. Instead, I just pointed at the wall and shook my head. Ratner started talking about something, but I tuned him out. As he yammered on about something in that pissed-off voice of his, I looked at the faded boards of that unmarked wall and wondered what on earth was happening to me. I refused to think I'd imagined my time in the shack two days before. Desperate, I examined my surroundings, searching for some clue that this might be a different shack, but the landscape was exactly as I remembered it. We were in the right place. The right place had changed, though.

"Let's get back," Davey said, and we started the climb out of the valley. I was too busy trying to make sense of things to protest.

"Not cut out for this kind of work," Ratner said. His voice was acidic. "Should've stayed a teacher or whatever."

Yeah, it was a petty slight, and it pissed me off. I still had the image of Mitchell's brains blown across the cabin floor though, so I kept my mouth shut and fought the urge to give him the side eye. A few weeks ago, Ratner had been a friend as well as a fellow soldier. Now, I was scared of him. Hard to believe he's the guy I used to drink beers with while we watched Sunday football.

A few times on the way back, I caught Ratner and Davey shooting me glances. Could be I'm not the only one who's scared. If one of them had led me on a similar goose chase, I'd worry about their sanity. Why shouldn't they worry about mine? Maybe they'll try to strap me down like they did Renee, tell me it's for my own good when really they're scared I'll hurt one of them.

Of course, things are worse now. Who knows what's going to happen.

When we got back to the cabin, Renee was sitting on the porch. Not a good sign. Again, she had blood on her hands and forearms. Again, she stared at nothing, her eyes almost dead above the seeping bandages that lined her mouth. At least she wasn't screaming. Davey shouted and aimed his weapon, motioned for Ratner and me to check out the cabin. We rushed onto the porch, giving Renee as wide a berth as we could, and through the door.

"Sidney!" She didn't answer, so I called her name again. My voice echoed through the cabin.

Ratner charged past me and down the hall. He entered the room where we'd tied down Renee, and I heard him groan. "Dammit," he said.

I knew by the sound of his voice that I didn't have to hurry. I could walk, and it wouldn't make a bit of difference. Hell, I could probably crawl, stopping halfway to take a short nap. Either way, Sidney was dead, and there wasn't anything for us to do but dig another hole.

When I stepped into the doorway, I examined the scene over Ratner's shoulder. A part of me thought I might see a room of thorn bushes again, but that wasn't the case. I really wish it had been.

If Sidney's face hadn't been largely untouched, I might not have recognized her. Her cheek and lips were swollen from what looked like a couple of nasty punches, but the real damage had been saved for her body. It looked like Renee had turned her inside-out, just opened up her belly and started yanking on all the goodies she found inside. Blood and flesh and organs stretched from one end of the bedroom to the other.

I could see Sidney's heart from the doorway. It was in the center of the floor, where Renee had secured it with a single nail. The hammer lay discarded a few feet away, blood drying on the handle. Something cold ran through me, but it vanished when Ratner spun around and shoved past me.

"Fucking psycho," he said as he stomped down the hall.

When I caught up to him, he was stepping onto the porch and pressing the barrel of his pistol to the base of Renee's skull. He shouted something, but I couldn't hear it over the sound of my thoughts.

She'd nailed it to the floor. Right to the floor.

Davey started shouting, too. He didn't sound angry like Ratner, though. Just confused and frightened. Still, I couldn't make out any words. Static filled my ears and my head. The lights were too bright, everything yellow and burning. And there was laughter somewhere. Dry and clicking chuckles that fell like stones through the white noise in my brain.

"*You are nothing.*"

Ratner and Davey fell silent, and the white noise in my skull dissipated like mist in a strong wind. I didn't recognize the voice—it was hollow and ragged, like someone speaking from deep in a cave—but I knew the source. Slowly, I stepped past Ratner and walked down the steps until I stood beside Davey. I looked up at Renee as her mouth opened and that voice tumbled out again.

"*You are nothing. You mean nothing. We are old, and we are all.*" Her eyes didn't move, just kept staring into the distance.

"Crazy bitch," Ratner said, pushing at her neck with his pistol. "Why'd you do it?"

"*We like fear. We like to see it and smell it. And we like to watch the light go out when we snuff it.*"

"You didn't just kill Sidney."

"*No. We had fun. We will have more fun. Before we snuff your lights, we will smell your fear like a field of wildflowers, and you will beg us to kill you.*"

She burst into motion before any of us could react, leaping from the porch. Ratner fired a shot that slammed into her back, but she didn't notice. She hit the ground and rushed Davey, charging on all fours like a bull. Angry grunts punctuated each step. Davey scurried toward the forest, but his hurried, backwards steps couldn't match her pace. She closed to within ten feet of him and leaped. I've seen videos of attacking tigers practically flying out of tall grass, and this looked like that.

Davey shot from the hip. The burst caught Renee in the chest and belly, ripping her from the air and leaving a red mist drifting down behind her. She didn't stop, though. As soon as she hit the ground, she sprang to all fours and charged again. Davey screamed and backed up a few more steps, but Renee pounced before he could squeeze off another shot. The rifle fell from his hands, and I saw Renee's nails sink into the soft flesh of his throat before she finished riding him to the dirt.

Ratner and I ran toward the pair. Maybe he had some idea what to do, but I was running on pure instinct. Nothing in my head resembled a plan. Renee hissed, and I heard this wet, tearing sound. Blood jetted into the air, and Davey's screams became gurgles.

I reached them first, and I threw a kick before I could even come to a stop. The toe of my boot hit Renee in the temple, and she fell to the side. She rolled into a crouch and hissed. Backing up, I lifted my hands to my throat.

A pair of shots rang out. One caught Renee in the neck, spraying crimson, and the other punched through her skull. She dropped and stayed down, thank God.

I dropped to my knees beside Davey. My plan was to search through the ruin of his throat for his carotid and pinch it off, but his glassy eyes told me it was already too late. His blood flow had already eased from a violent surge to a weak trickle. He was gone.

From my knees, I watched as Ratner walked across the yard to stand over Renee's body. He pumped three more bullets into her head. I didn't even care how much the shots made my ears hurt.

Neither of us wanted to dig another grave, so we dragged their bodies into the woods and left them. We shut the door to the room where Sidney died.

Maybe we'll try to give all of them a burial tomorrow. I think we might just dig one big hole and put all three inside. It's not the most respectful idea, but I'm so tired of digging. Pretty sure Ratner is, too.

August 24ᵗʰ

Long talk with Ratner today. We should have been burying bodies, but neither of us has the strength or desire. Instead, we discussed leaving, just ditching the safe house and scattering to the winds. No orders had come in, but it wasn't as though we still had a full team. Like it or not, we had to admit our usefulness was pretty much screwed.

We sat on the couch, the same place Davey had wrestled Renee's hands from her face, and passed a bottle of bourbon back and forth. Because why not? We'd checked the news, and things were bad. Lot of our folks getting rounded up. For all we could figure, the feds might know about our cabin.

"I wonder if Jenny's okay," I said. "Her and the kids...I told them I was running out when I came up here. Followed the protocols to the letter, right? Now, I just want to know she's all right. I want to hear her voice, even if it's just her calling me an asshole."

Ratner took a pull of the bottle and frowned as he smiled. "Yeah, that would be nice. Told 'em you were skipping out, huh?"

"Uh-huh. You told your wife something different?"

For a long stretch of seconds, he didn't answer. He sat beside me, motionless as a corpse. When he finally moved, it was to lift the bottle to his lips again. "Um, no. I mean yeah. Sure, I told her the same thing."

"Mitchell should've done that."

"Yeah. Guess you're right about that."

The bottle appeared in my hand, and I took a healthy swallow. Liquor burned a path down my throat and settled into my belly. The world canted to one side and then righted itself. "I think I'm going to go home tomorrow," I said.

"Fuck the orders we don't have, right?"

"Pretty much, yeah. It's the last couple of days, y'know? Really messed up the way I look at all this. I don't want to wait until we hit zero and then go see if Jenny and the kids are okay. I want to know now, and I want to fix things."

"Fixing things is good," Ratner said. "Got a few things I wouldn't mind fixing."

"You can. Not like one person can do a job two can't."

"You got a point, buddy. Got a real good point." Grunting, he leaned forward and then stood on unsteady legs. He stretched, and I heard his backbone pop in a few places. "I'm going for a walk."

"I don't think—"

"Going for a walk. Don't worry about it." And then he stumbled out the front door and into the night.

I sat on the couch for a long time, my hand growing limp around the bottle's neck. My head felt soft and heavy, and the shadows in the cabin's living room writhed over the walls. With each passing minute, my eyelids grew heavier. I thought about Ratner, about what he might have meant and if he was safe alone, but I couldn't seem to get off my ass and go after him. All I wanted was my bed.

The bottle in my fist, I climbed off the couch and shambled toward my bedroom. A bad smell filled the hallway, and I remembered Sidney stretched across the room at the end of the hall. I decided that once I woke up and shook off what would be a terrible hangover, I'd decide to either clean the room or leave. I think leaving's the best choice.

I'm not sure why, but I went to the end of the hall and placed a hand on the door. In my head, I saw Sidney's ruined body, saw her dead eyes stare at the ceiling. She didn't deserve such a fate. When we signed on, we knew death was an option, but there's a big difference between being martyred by the government and being ripped to pieces by a psycho.

Squeezing my eyes shut, I leaned forward and rested my forehead against the door. Was Renee a psycho? A part of me wanted to say so, but the rest of me thought about that shack and the heart nailed inside the dresser, the mad impacts and scrabbling of something trying to break in. I'd been in the woods a couple of hours and experienced that. Renee had been out longer than a day. What if something got to her? Changed her?

We are old, and we are all.

A shiver ran through me as I remembered the words and the voice that spoke them. I was still thinking about the voice when I heard another sound, something soft and rhythmic, keeping steady, determined time on the other side of the door. My eyes watered, and tears spilled down my cheeks. I whined, but the sound wouldn't stop. Even in pieces, even with her heart nailed to the floor, Sidney's pulse was strong.

Last Day

I don't know how much time I have (probably not long), so I'll write as quickly as I can. Yeah, I'm that asshole, the one who should leave but keeps writing instead. Trust me, I'd leave if it was an option. The banging on the door says otherwise. That scrabbling is back, too. It tells me it's not the FBI or even the state police. I really wish it was one or the other.

I was packing my bag to leave when the first impact slammed into the front door. So at least I can say I was trying to leave. I'm not that idiot.

Didn't see anything when I looked out the windows, not that I expected to. All the vehicles are still outside, but there's no sign of Ratner. I'm guessing his walk didn't turn out well.

Shit. Just heard the door splinter. Not much time at all.

We are old, and we are all.

I don't know what that means, but I think I'll find out soon.

I love you, Jenny. I love you and the kids, and I'm so sorry I had to lie to you.

The door just broke apart. Scrabbling on my bedroom door now.

We were supposed to be heroes. Save the whole damn country. Didn't work out so well.

Reaching zero. Here it comes.

Goodbye.

PEEKING THROUGH THE CLOUDS:

AN AFTERWORD AND STORY NOTES

by Nate Southard

So, here we are. I hope you enjoyed yourself. If you didn't, I hope you have the decency to keep it to yourself. Lie to your friends; tell them you loved it. I'll give you a dollar.

Of course, I don't mind telling you folks the truth, even when it's ugly. In the spring of 2014, I was just about done. At that point, I'd been publishing almost ten years. Now, if you ask a great writer—or a great comedian, chef, athlete, etcetera—they'll say you spend the first decade of your chosen vocation pretty much sucking. You're still building your chops and finding your voice, paying your dues as you lay the foundation for the pitiful, broken existence you'll eventually call *Your Career*. I knew I was coming up on the end of that, and I knew I was heads and shoulders better than I'd been back in 2004.

The only problem was I was still positive I sucked. Hard.

I was on my way to Norman, Oklahoma with my friends Shane McKenzie and Gabino Iglesias for a Noir at the Bar event. The drive up was great, because Shane and Gabino are great company. We listened to standup comedy the entire way and created a running joke about Carl's Jr, ham sandwiches, and fried pies that kept us in stitches for seven hours (trust me...you had to be there). What they didn't know was that I was pretty sure this would be my last hurrah, a quick reading to promote my crime novel *Pale Horses*, and then I would quit. I still didn't think my writing was any good, and the endlessly frustrating cycle of *write novel, try to land agent, fail to land agent, try to find publisher, maybe find publisher, try to promote book when bookstores won't stock said book* was wearing me down.

And the thing was, I knew that was the game. I never lost sight of that. You suck for ten years, and, if you're lucky, you come out of those ten years sucking a little less. Part of the problem was that I'd spent the past several years dealing with serious depression issues. Another part was my growing envy of Shane, who seemed to succeed at everything he decided to try (look...I'm an asshole, and I'm petty). Seriously, last week he said he wanted to try standup comedy. I look forward to his first HBO special, coming sometime shortly after Christmas, I'm sure.

But I digress. The point is, I was sad and broken and exhausted, and I didn't want to do this shit anymore. The fact that I'd started referring to writing as *This Shit* is probably the most indicative thing I've written so far. So, I'd go to Norman, read the first chapter of *Pale Horses*, go sleep in the hotel, and then drive back the next morning and start my new life without *This Shit*. Or at least without the mountain of self-pity I seemed to be carrying around.

Then, I met J. David Osborne, owner/head honcho of Broken River Books. James had set up the Norman event, and exuded this strange kind of casual enthusiasm. It took me a while to catch on that there was anything else going on beside him just being a nice guy, but once I did, I was infected by it. He believed in this event, and I wanted to do right by him. Shit, I wanted to impress him. Back in high school, I was in a band, one of those mediocre cover bands that you're sure is amazing at the time. As we all hung out in this Oklahoma dive bar, waiting to start our readings, I started to feel like the guy who'd been the drummer in that band, the guy who, when setting up his drums in a friend's basement or barn, has a single, all-powerful goal in mind: *let's put on a goddamn show.*

I decided that, in addition to reading the first chapter of *Pale Horses*, I'd read the first part of a story called "The Broken Ballad of Dr. Fantastic." Serving as the middle chapter of my novel *The Slab City Event*, "Dr. Fantastic" is a pretty transparent stand-in for Hunter S. Thompson, and the story follows what happens when zombies attack the squat where he's living in the middle of the desert. Let's be clear…it's a ridiculous story. It's a fun one, however, full of all sorts of interesting language and phrasing, so I decided to read it.

And I read the shit out of it. I threw a lot into that reading, riding those words like waves. For the first time, something to do with writing was fun again, and it was because I wanted to show this quietly enthusiastic guy that I got it, that I was there to have a good time and help in any way I could.

When I stepped away from the mic, I received more applause than I've ever experienced in my life. Osborne grabbed the mic and said something like, "Man, what the hell was *that?*"

What was it? It was the best I could do. And the least I could do. Because when we realize we love writing, that we love the process of creating, the best we can do is the very least we owe the world. Me? I love writing again. So I'll keep doing my best. Shit, it's the least I can do.

STORY NOTES

He Stepped Through

The last season of *The Shield* remains, in my mind, one of the greatest single seasons in the history of television. There's so much happening in those final episodes, and the tension just keeps ratcheting higher and higher.

Early in the season, however, there were a few scenes that really snagged my imagination. One was the house filled with bodies, and the other was the body that got dragged down the street, leaving a long smear of blood. In the show, they're both used as examples of escalating violence in the community, but I kept coming back to the idea that it might be cool if they were part of something greater. Imagine if that last season of *The Shield* kept getting darker and darker, and then the last scene goes full-blown supernatural. Okay, so there would have been a million cries of bullshit, but I would have dug the hell out of it.

So I wrote *He Stepped Through*. Bloodletting Books released it as a chapbook back in 2010, and I've been looking for the right way to re-release it.

For this book, I made some pretty massive rewrites to *He Stepped Through*. Most notably, the original version of this story was pretty blatantly Lovecraftian, complete with Cthulhu and Nyarlathotep references and lots of sentences that were mostly consonants. Now, there's nothing wrong with that, but a few years ago I wrote a novel, *Down*, that introduced something called The Darkness Below. Ever since, I'd kept kicking around the idea of expanding on that idea. I'm still not sure I want to pull the trigger and call it a full-blown mythos, but I'm very much enjoying playing around with The Darkness Below and seeing what I can do with it.

Something Went Wrong

In 2011, I went through a breakup. It wasn't a bad breakup with lots of screaming or anything. To tell the truth, my ex is still my best friend. At the time, however, it felt like the end of the world. After eleven years, we'd fallen apart, and both of us felt like that meant we'd failed at life in some fundamental way. If you've never experienced it, I don't know how to explain it to you. It big and horrible and it takes over your entire life.

Obviously, this plays a big part in the story. I needed to work through some things, so I did. The rest of the story is an interesting patchwork of other ideas I'd had over the years. The body parts left in paper bags stuff has been in my head since 2006, and I just hadn't been able to make it fit anywhere else. There was also a restaurant on Lake Travis called Carlos and Charlie's that ended up going out of business after a years-long draught. They were still clinging to life when I first wrote this.

Both this and *He Stepped Through* are good examples of the kind of stories I really enjoy. I like when there are several plot threads that weave in and out of each other until you realize it's all telling the same story. Sometimes it doesn't work, but, when it does, it's a thrill. Hopefully, these worked for you.

Deeper Waters

Meet Charlie Crawford. Redneck. Asshole. Magician. I'm not sure he's my favorite creation, but he's easily in the top three. As I write this, I'm putting the finishing touches on what I hope will be the first of several Charlie Crawford novels. Time will tell. This was his first story, and he's a little different here than he eventually became in my head. I won't say Charlie is currently kinder and gentler, but I will say he has a few more issues than he shows here.

The idea for the flood came from my hometown of Aurora, Indiana, which I don't mind admitting was the inspiration for Sulfer. It sits right on a bend in the Ohio River, and it flooded really bad a few years before I moved to Texas. In the early part of the 20th century, however, the river smothered the entire town, water rising to the second story windows along First, Second, and Third Streets. In the neighboring town of Lawrenceburg, there are several spots in town where you can see the tops of windows peeking over the sidewalk. My third grade teacher told us this was because, after the big flood, it was decided it would be easier to toss everything that was ruined into the streets and raise the street level eight feet. I don't know how true that is, but I hope it isn't a complete fabrication.

Safe House

In the summer of 2013, Michael McBride and Thunderstorm Books publisher Paul Goblirsch contacted me about co-editing an anthology to celebrate Thunderstorm's 100th release. I agreed, and a few months later Mike and I birthed

Mia Moja, where this novella originally appeared. The idea behind the antho, that it would contain Thunderstorm's ten most prolific authors, meant Mike and I had to appear in it, despite our hemming and hawing over the idea. I'm glad we gave in, because I was very pleased with the story that came out of it.

Again, I'd wanted to tell an epistolary story about a group of militia members hiding out in the woods for some time. Originally, I'd thought it might be a novel-length story called *The Revolution Diaries*, but I think it works a lot better at this length. Even then, I took three different stabs at it before I found the right way to pull off *Safe House*. Those first attempts were a little too…well, they sucked. How's that?

We also see a little bit more of The Darkness Below in this one. That sucker's everywhere, huh? I think there's some solid potential in that idea. Pretty sure you'll see more of it down the line.

Take care, folks.

Nate Southard
October, 2014

ACKNOWLEDGEMENTS

The sad fact of the matter is, no matter how hard I try to remember everybody I owe a serious thanks to, I'm going to forget somebody. If you're someone I end up forgetting, I'm sorry. Please don't hate me.

First off, thanks to J. David Osborne for both bringing this collection to life and for letting me give it a long and ridiculous title. You rule so damn hard.

Thank you so much to Laird Barron for the wonderful introduction.

Thanks to Paul Goblirsch and Larry Roberts, who published the original editions of these novellas.

A special round of thank you's to my friends who keep me sane and remain my friends despite my flakey, anti-social behavior: Shawna Blount, Lee Thomas, Sheresa Edgington, Cole Latimer, Chris Nicholas, Michael Barnes, David Lamplugh, Ek Timrerk, Marilyn Nguyen, Thanh Ong, Alyssa Blount, Wrath James White, Ed Kurtz, Michael Louis Dixon, and Tristan Thorne.

And finally, a most sincere thanks to Shane McKenzie and Gabino Iglesias. First fried pie is on me.

ABOUT THE AUTHOR

Nate Southard is the author of *Down, Pale Horses, Just Like Hell,* and several others. His work has appeared in such venues as *Cemetery Dance, Black Static,* and *Thuglit.* A finalist for the Bram Stoker Award for Superior Achievement in Short Fiction, Nate lives in Austin, Texas with his best friend and two cats. He cooks a lot. Learn more at natesouthard.com.